# Every Witch Way but Frosty

Magical Misfits Mysteries - book 16

## K.E. O'Connor

K.E. O'Connor Books

EVERY WITCH WAY BUT FROSTY

Copyright © 2023 by K.E. O'Connor

ISBN: 978-1-915378-87-3

Written by: K.E. O'Connor.

# Chapter 1

# Good hunting

"How do you walk about without treading on your tail?" My wonderful witch, Zandra Crypt, grabbed the enormous white fluffy tail that was part of her Yuletide costume and glared at it.

I was perched comfortably on the end of her bed in our basement room, stifling laughter as she struggled to get comfortable in her oversized cat costume. "It would help if you were on your hands and knees. You're too upright to have a tail."

"I'm not doing this freezing cold hunt crawling around in the snow. We won't last five minutes." Zandra tossed the tail over one shoulder. It fell off and hit the floor with a thud. "And I'm determined we're winning that food hamper. Did you see the size of the honeyed ham?"

"It is quite the prize," I agreed.

Zandra stomped into the bathroom, where she peered at herself in the mirror. She'd been stomping about a lot recently.

I hopped off the bed and joined her, perching with precision on the edge of the sink. "Is that all you're worried about?"

"Have you seen the list of people taking part in the witch hunt? We've got stiff competition." Zandra adjusted her fluffy white ears.

"We'll outmatch all of them. We're the best team in town."

"If you say so."

A twinge of anxiety pinged in my stomach. Things had been more than a little strained between us ever since Crimson Cove got turned on its head by my devious nemesis, who'd been hiding as a familiar in order to weave trouble throughout our home. Zandra had been taken from me, whisked away, along with the stones that stored much of my ancient magic. And when she returned, I should have revealed everything about the stones, my true power, and why a demigoddess had wanted me to join her, but I still hesitated.

I knew what the problem was. I feared Zandra might reject me when she learned what I used to be. My demigoddess days seemed a long time ago, but being confronted by my past was a harsh reminder that powerful enemies always loomed. And I'd gotten so used to being a stunning white cat with a delightful witch sidekick that, if I released the magic in the stones, maybe I'd be unable to adjust. Maybe Zandra wouldn't be able to adjust at all. Having lost her once, I was reluctant to lose her again. And that was the risk I'd be taking by revealing everything.

"If we're going to be a part of this hunt, we need to get a move on," Zandra said. "It starts at dusk."

"We're doing it, and we'll win." I followed Zandra back into the converted basement in Vorana Stowell's cozy house. "Are you sure there's nothing else on your mind? You've been agitated ever since you got a message on your snow globe. Was it bad news?"

Zandra flipped her dark hair out of her face. "It's not bad news exactly. But it is stressful news. For both of us."

"Don't tell me Barney wants us to work over the holidays?" I asked. "We've booked the week off, and I have plans to catch up on sleep and snacking."

Zandra smirked. "Me, too. It's not work. Ever since you dealt with Nimbus, animal control has quietened down again. There's even been a few days when I was bored. And it's been a long time since I've felt that."

"You're not still thinking of making a change, are you?" I asked. "We like animal control, don't we?"

"Sure, our job is fine. And you know that wasn't me talking when I said I wanted to leave all this behind." Zandra gestured around the room.

"I know. It was the troublesome fungi talking."

"I'll never underestimate the humble mushroom ever again," Zandra said.

I nodded. "If it's not work causing you an issue, then what is it?"

Zandra heaved a sigh. "The message was from Tempest. She wants to visit over the holidays."

"That's excellent news, not stressful," I said. "Will she bring Wiggles?"

"Where my grouchy half-sister goes, Wiggles goes, too, so you'll have to put up with him hanging around," Zandra said.

"I thought Wiggles couldn't leave Willow Tree Falls. The magic keeping him as a mini magical hellhound only stretches so far."

"Apparently, Tempest treated Wiggles to an early present. A spell, so he can leave Willow Tree Falls for a short time."

"I don't mind Wiggles. And it's been too long since you and Tempest have been together," I said. "You have a lot to catch up on."

"I guess." Zandra glanced around the basement. "What will Tempest think of this, though? It's not as if we're living the high life. I only ever planned on staying in Vorana's basement temporarily until I sorted things out, but we're still here."

"Why would we ever want to leave?" I asked. "The basement is wonderfully warm. Vorana is a dear friend. And she makes us marvelous food."

"But Tempest has her own place! And she runs her own business."

"Tempest has an apartment above a noisy bar that keeps her busy into the small hours," I said.

"She shares a house with her boyfriend, too. And that place is huge."

"You know Tempest. She has no interest in material things," I said. "So long as she sees you're happy, she won't mind where you're living. It could be under a bridge, provided you're content."

"I just want her to be proud of me." Zandra made a valiant attempt at tucking the tail into the top of her costume. It fell to the floor again.

"Your whole family is proud of you," I said. "Will Tempest and Wiggles stay with us while they're here?"

"That's the plan. Tempest left it too late to book anywhere, so the hotels are full." Zandra headed to the stairs.

"There's room down here. You can share the bed with Tempest or use a blow-up mattress on the floor." I wrinkled my booping snooter. "We'll have to crack a window, though. Wiggles is a pungent little guy."

"We'll have to put up with the smell. It's freezing outside, and they're predicting more snow, so the window stays shut."

I trotted up the stairs after Zandra. "He won't mind sleeping outside. After all, he always burns too hot. That's hellhounds for you."

"Tempest will have a thing or two to say about that. They usually share a bed." Zandra walked into the kitchen, and we discovered Vorana dressed as a giant version of her familiar, Sage. She'd even painted whiskers and an adorable black nose on her face.

She caught one look at Zandra and laughed. "You should have gone down a size. Your Juno outfit swamps you."

"I bought it online!" Zandra said. "It was one size fits all. I didn't know the sizing related to ogres."

Vorana's outfit was perfectly tailored, hugging her curves and making her look like the perfect cat woman. Or rather, witch-like version of Sage.

"I forgot this was your first Yuletide witch hunt," Vorana said. "I should have taken you shopping.

Everyone makes such an effort with their costumes, so we don't let our familiars down. Not that you've let Juno down, of course. It's just..."

Zandra scowled at the hefty white tail. "I know. The costume is terrible. I'll be a joke."

"My witch always does everything perfectly," I said, although as I eyed the oversized white cat costume, I made a mental note to ensure next year, Zandra looked less yeti and more slinky white snow leopard.

Crimson Cove's Yuletide annual witch hunt was a fun festive celebration, where magic users dressed as their familiars and we chased them through the woods. The rules were simple. We weren't allowed to use magic, and we couldn't chase our own bonded magic user. The last pair standing won the grand hamper prize of food. Lots and lots of yummy, festive food.

Sage trundled into the kitchen in her harness and bumped against me. "Don't think you're winning this prize."

"It had crossed my mind," I said.

She hissed softly at me. "I won two Christmases ago, and I intend to win back the top spot."

"Your efforts will be valiant, but with us involved, they'll end in failure."

"They'll be the winning effort." Her hackles lifted. Sage was taking this hunt seriously.

In the spirit of the season, I offered a sprig of mistletoe. "How about this? If either of us wins, we'll share. The hamper is enormous, so there's enough food to keep us satisfied for weeks."

Sage grunted in her usual curmudgeonly way. "I'll consider sharing. Only with you, though."

"And Vorana."

"That goes without saying."

"And Zandra?"

"I'll think about it."

"We could work together," I suggested. "Really put the competition's noses out of joint."

"No collaborations, you two! It's against the rules." Vorana turned to Zandra. "Let me pin your tail onto your back. You don't want to trip and faceplant into the snow."

Once Zandra's tail was securely pinned, we left the house and walked down the freshly swept steps. Snow had been falling for a week, although not always heavily, but enough to leave several inches on the ground. The heavy yellow clouds that loomed overhead as dusk fell promised more snow was on its way. We were definitely having a white Christmas.

Zandra and Vorana walked ahead, following a trail of people marching toward Crimson Cove woods to take part in the hunt.

Sage lifted her chin. "Have you fixed things with Zandra yet?"

"I didn't realize there was anything to fix."

She slid me a glare. "I know you haven't told her the truth."

"I never lie to my witch."

"About your stones! You keep dodging the responsibility."

I stared straight ahead. When we'd almost lost the town and our magic users because of my nemesis's bad behavior, I'd used some of my old magic to ensure Zandra's safety. She'd gotten a boost of my ancient power and, ever since, had wanted to know about the stones that stored my magic. We'd had a few surface conversations, but I'd yet to reveal it was my trapped demigoddess magic, and Zandra now had some of it running through her veins, and more than a tiny amount.

"Ignoring me and the situation won't solve things," Sage said.

"I'm not ignoring you. I'm thinking," I said. "Such a delicate situation requires a lengthy timeframe and a well-considered plan."

"You're scared."

"Nothing scares me."

"Of what Zandra will think of you," Sage said. "I'd be the same if the situations were reversed and I had a giant, life-altering, terrifying secret hanging over my head that I needed to tell Vorana."

"I'll get around to it," I said. "But not today. I don't want to spoil Christmas."

"There was plenty of time before the festive season rolled around to deal with this," Sage said.

"I am dealing with it! All good things come to those who wait."

"Throwing trite sayings at me won't get you out of this," Sage said.

She was right, and I'd needed a temporary fix before I got my magical stones lined up and revealed everything. That fix had come in the form of a brown leather bracelet I'd given Zandra as an early Christmas gift. The bracelet contained a tiny amount of magic, which ensured Zandra lost interest in asking about the stones and focused on more important things. Like tickling me under my chin and remembering to feed me my second breakfast.

Was it the right thing to do? Some would say not. Some would even say it was morally gray. But I needed breathing space. If my life with Zandra was about to change, I had to make preparations and figure out how things would work once she knew the whole truth about me.

At least, that was what I was telling myself, and I was sticking to that story until a better one came along. One with a guaranteed happy ending.

"Where did those angels come from?" Sage asked. "They're not our regular bunch of feathered buffoons. I don't know any of them."

As we arrived at the edge of Crimson Cove woods, we discovered a handful of new angels in attendance. They were dressed as either cats or dogs. A second later, Cythera and Bertoli joined them, and I was thrilled to see they were also in costume. Cythera wore a spotted black and white dog costume, and Bertoli was a pale ginger cat.

"I didn't know the angels took part in the hunt," I said. "Is that allowed? They can't bond with a familiar, so they don't have a team mate to play with."

"There's always an Angel Force presence," Sage said. "Things can get rough, so they need to keep order without standing out and spoiling the fun."

I turned my attention to the group of angels they'd joined. "Those angels know Cythera."

"Family? Could be from Maverick's side," Sage said.

"I don't think so. At least they didn't attend the wedding." I trotted over and stopped in front of Cythera and her friends. "Greetings! I'm disappointed you didn't dress like a cat. You'd have made a magnificent feline. You're joining in the hunt?"

She glanced down at me, and her nose wrinkled. "This event brings out the worst in people. I'm here to make sure there's no bloodshed. We don't want a repeat of last year."

"What happened last year?"

"Ask someone else." She turned away.

I batted her solid calf with a hard paw. "Your friends are taking part, too? We've not been introduced."

"They're my friends!" Bertoli said with a big smile. "Crimson Cove is hosting the Academy's annual reunion, and these angels are from my graduating class. This is Habriel. Sorush. Tabris. Nisroc, Arioch, and Virgil."

"It's good to meet you all," I said. "I often assist Bertoli with his most vexing cases. Cythera, too."

"Don't you have a magic user to chase?" Cythera flipped her fake tail at me.

"We're not starting for five minutes," I said. "Will I get to hunt you?"

"If you lay one paw on me, you'll regret it."

"You can hunt us if you like," said the largest of the angels who'd been introduced as Habriel. He was dressed in a shaggy gray dog costume. He was the vision of angelic perfection, although his eyes were an unusually deep shade of blue. Most angels had pale blue eyes that looked almost alien in certain lights. "When we heard about the annual hunt, we begged to take part. It sounds like fun."

"Welcome to Crimson Cove," I said. "It's my first time taking part, too."

Habriel puffed out his fuzzy chest. "I'm the fastest of this group. I always won the track medals at the Academy."

"You were a blur when you ran." Sorush grinned at his friend. "We never stood a chance against you."

Habriel slung his arm around the other angel's shoulders. "I almost let you beat me once."

There was a shrill whistle, which was the signal for us to get ready. Laughter filled the air as over fifty magic users dressed in their costumes got ready to bolt through the trees. They got a five-minute head start before we pursued them, so I left the angels and settled in beside Sage to enjoy soaking up the cheery atmosphere.

"I'm going after one of the angels first," Sage whispered. "I can never resist batting at those feathers."

"They'll be fast. They could cause us trouble," I said. "That big one with the loud voice is clearly the leader of the group, so watch out for him."

"I recognize him from somewhere," Sage said. "And he looks different from the others. More polished."

"I've never met an angel who wasn't put together and almost so good-looking they were painful to observe."

Cythera marched toward the waiting magic users, got them into order, and then stood to the side. She raised an arm. The whistle blew again, and they all shot off, talking, joking, and good-naturedly shoving each other.

I twitched with excitement. It was always fun chasing prey, no matter its size. I kept watch on which direction Zandra raced off, pleased to see her getting ahead of the pack. The odds of winning were on our side.

Sage was on her paws, her pupils dilated, and her ears lowered. "Let the hunt begin!"

And what a hunt it would be.

# Chapter 2

## Run and hide

The frosty air and occasional flurries of snow filtering through the tree branches did nothing to dampen my excitement. We were twenty minutes into the hunt, and I'd already caught five magic users, eliminating them from the competition. I felt Zandra was still in the running, literally running, so that hamper was ever closer to becoming ours.

I lifted my booping snooter and inhaled deeply. There was a familiar cinnamon sugar scent in the air that meant only one thing. An angel was close by, and I intended to bring him down and shred a few white feathers.

Sage had darted off in pursuit of her own angel, so I was alone as I crept through the woods, carefully avoiding the crunchy leaves that might give away my location and cause my prey to bolt.

The sweet smell grew stronger, and I stopped to listen for sounds that would reveal my target. A small groan hit my ears, and I hurried toward it. Sitting on the ground, holding one ankle, was Nisroc, one of Bertoli's angel friends.

His head whipped up as I bounded toward him, and he held up one hand. "I admit defeat. You don't need to jump on me."

I slowed and took in the situation. "You've hurt yourself?"

"Something like that," Nisroc said. "One of my friends got overexcited and shoved me out of the way. My foot landed in a hole, and I twisted my ankle."

"That's unangel-like behavior." I eyed him. Nisroc was a small angel with narrow hips and shoulders. Most male angels were typically Adonis-like, but he looked more like a long-distance runner.

There was a yelp close by, followed by a grunt, as another contestant was taken out.

"I didn't think this hunt would be so brutal," Nisroc said. "It reminds me of our old school games. It was always a case of the last one standing, especially when it came to dodgeball. I lost two teeth during a game."

"That sounds deeply unpleasant," I said.

"Is your magic user still in the hunt?" Nisroc asked.

"Naturally. I'm bonded to the most wonderful witch you'll ever meet. Zandra Crypt."

He nodded. "I know of the Crypt witches, by reputation only. My aunt is friends with the angel who runs Angel Force in Willow Tree Falls. She often hears elaborate tales about the Crypt witches and their demon prison. It's something special. They're something special."

"They're a unique coven," I said. "Let me check your ankle to make sure you can walk on it."

Nisroc shied away as I got closer. "Careful! It really hurts."

"I know healing spells that will help you. I'll be gentle."

Nisroc let me sniff his ankle, and once I was certain it wasn't broken, I got him to test his weight on it.

He grimaced. "It'll be a slow walk back."

"It doesn't need to be. If you'll allow me to help?" I gestured with a paw toward his ankle.

"Thanks. That's decent of you. Only if it's no trouble. I hate being a problem. I always seem to find myself in the way and making a nuisance of myself."

"It's no less than any of your friends would do for you." I cast a basic healing spell, and within a couple of moments, Nisroc was twisting his ankle around, no longer grunting with discomfort.

"If you want to head back to the start, I believe those who don't make it to the end are rewarded with hot chocolate and iced brownies while we wait for the winner to emerge," I said.

"That's just what I need." Nisroc's gaze flashed around the trees. "I can't believe you do this every year in the freezing cold."

"It's chilly but fun," I said.

He briskly rubbed his arms. "I'll head back and see if anyone else in my party's been caught. I hope I'm not the first. I won't hear the end of it if I am. The others will tease me all night."

"Good luck. And watch out for any more holes."

Nisroc raised a hand as he headed off into the darkness.

I fluffed out my fur. It was frigid out, but I was determined to win this hunt. I crept deeper into the woods, no longer hearing people being pursued. We must be down to the last few prey. I wanted to check in with Zandra, but magic wasn't permitted, and I didn't want us to be kicked out of the contest because of an error on my part.

The darkness grew more intense, and a chill wind blasted past me. I was tempted to give up and follow Nisroc. I could sit on his lap while he drank his hot chocolate and wait for Zandra to return victorious.

I cocked my head, my senses on high alert. There was someone behind me. There was no point in stalking me! I wasn't the prey in this hunt. I pretended not to have heard and kept walking. Whoever it was, they matched my steps, paw for paw. Clever.

What game was being played?

I ducked behind a large pine tree and waited for my stalker to approach. I took several deep, calming breaths, hearing them edge closer. When they were within paw-striking distance, I leapt out, murder mittens at the ready, and landed on a hot furry back. There was a howl, and a blast of fire illuminated the trees, dazzling in its intensity. Then we were rolling, over and over, as more fire poured out of my unsuspecting victim.

I sank my claws into a thick scruff and gave it a shake. I recognized that taste! I let go and hissed, "Wiggles! I should have known your unique stink."

"Get those claws out of my belly! They sting." He howled and tried to shake me loose.

I unlatched my murder mittens and rolled onto my paws, shaking dried leaves out of my fur. "Don't you know the rules of the game? I'm a hunter! You don't chase me."

"I wasn't hunting you. Well, just for a few minutes. It was meant to be a surprise." Wiggles was a short, stout, miniature hellhound, who was currently investigating the puncture marks I'd inflicted on him. He'd once been a regular dog, but after an unfortunate incident with a car, he'd been magicked into an immortal, almost all-powerful, tiny hellhound with an unfortunate lingering scent and a fierce devotion to Tempest.

"I am surprised." I narrowed my eyes. "Is Tempest taking part, too?"

"Of course she is! She loves a challenge."

"That was why you were stalking me!" I hissed my displeasure. "Don't think Tempest will win. There's tough competition in these woods. Crimson Cove's residents aren't to be messed with."

"Neither are Willow Tree Falls' residents." Wiggles puffed out a plume of smoke and licked at his belly. "And I've seen the size of that hamper. We're winning it."

"It'll be a Christmas miracle if you do." I checked my fur wasn't too rumpled and then gently patted his muzzle with a velvet paw. "It's good to see you, old friend. I didn't know you were expected so soon."

He wagged his tail, falling into step with me as we walked through the woods. "Tempest decided to visit a day early. The rest of the family was driving her crazy with all the demands to put up the Christmas decorations."

"What about the bar? Cloven Hoof is always busy this time of year."

"Tempest has taken a step back from that," Wiggles said. "She hired more staff, so we have free time. But when Granny Dottie insisted Tempest decorate the entire house, including the outside, she made excuses and said we were needed here."

"Zandra will be surprised." And it wouldn't be a happy surprise. If there was one thing my witch despised, it was surprises.

"We also arrived early because of the party." Wiggles stopped to eat something off the forest floor.

"What party?" I asked.

"The angels are having some fancy get together." Wiggles continued along the path with me, still chewing. "I don't know much about it. I was half asleep when Tempest was telling me. Some big do, so there'll be food."

"If it's a party for angels, you won't be invited," I said.

"Tempest has an in with the angels," Wiggles said. "She'll get an invitation. And if she doesn't, we'll sneak in anyway. The angels always do an amazing buffet."

"Good luck with that. You've not met the angel who's in charge in Crimson Cove, have you?"

"They're all the same. They waggle their feathers, but it's all hot air and sparkles."

I couldn't resist a smirk. Cythera wasn't to be trifled with, so I'd enjoy seeing Tempest and Cythera lock horns while Wiggles assisted.

There was a startled yelp, and a blast of magic lit the trees. Instantly, I was off. I recognized the magic signature and that yelp. It came from Zandra.

Wiggles was hot on my heels. "I thought we weren't supposed to use magic to bring down prey?"

"We're not. It's an instant disqualification. Zandra would only pull out a spell in an emergency." I tugged on our bond, but it was strong and healthy, so she wasn't in critical danger.

As we reached the location where the magic had blasted out from, I discovered Habriel restraining Zandra on the ground. He had a knee pressed into her back and one arm around her throat, his face contorted with concentration as he tried to keep her down. Zandra's eyes glowed with fury, and the air crackled with the remnants of her spell, but Habriel seemed determined to subdue her.

Without hesitation, I sprang forward, my paws skimming the forest floor as I closed the distance.

Habriel barely had time to react as I launched myself at him. With a furious yowl, I sunk my claws into his shoulder and dragged him off Zandra. He let out a sharp grunt, surprised by the sudden assault.

Zandra twisted and threw Habriel off balance. She rolled out from under him, gasping for air, her hands glowing with gathering magic.

Habriel recovered quickly, his wings unfurling in a flash of white. But I wasn't letting him get the upper hand again. I darted in front of Zandra, baring my teeth, accompanied by a warning hiss so loud it made the leafless branches quiver.

"Stay back!" I snarled. My fur bristled as I faced off against Habriel.

He hesitated, his deep blue eyes narrowing as he assessed the situation. "Move aside. I intend to win this. And that witch stands in my way."

Zandra rose to her feet behind me, her magic flaring brighter. "You're breaking the rules. Prey doesn't attack prey."

"My witch is right, as always." My tail lashed behind me. "You're out of line."

Habriel's jaw tightened, and he lifted his hands, magic rippling across them. Zandra thrust her fists forward, releasing a blast that sent him stumbling.

With a swift leap, I landed squarely on Habriel's chest, knocking him to the ground. I pressed my murder mittens against his throat. There was a lot of sharp claw ready to draw blood. One of them may have sunk in.

"What are you doing, putting your hands on my witch?" I hissed into his face.

"She's prey," he wheezed out, his voice strained under the pressure of my paws.

"So are you," I growled back. "Prey doesn't attack prey."

His brow furrowed, and he opened his mouth to argue, but Zandra stepped closer, her magic still crackling around her. "You idiot! I'm out of the competition because of you."

"You didn't have to blast out a spell!" Habriel shot back.

I pressed my claws in a little harder, forcing him to stay still. "You're not in a position to argue. Apologize to Zandra."

He stared up at me, clearly reluctant to back down. When he didn't respond, I pressed harder, making him wince.

"Weren't you?" I demanded, my voice low and threatening.

Before Habriel could answer, pounding footsteps approached, and Tempest appeared, slightly breathless, her cheeks flushed with the cold. She was dressed a bit like Wiggles, with floppy ears on a headband and an oversized brown woolen coat, although she still had on her trademark black jeans and boots.

"What are you doing here?" Zandra was clearly surprised to see her.

"Visiting you!" Tempest's gaze flicked from Habriel to me. "I caught your magic signature and thought you might need a hand."

"We have everything under control," I said, keeping my eyes locked on Habriel. "This angel made a mistake, and he was just about to apologize for it."

Habriel's resistance faltered, and he sighed in defeat. "Fine, I'm sorry."

I eased off him, letting him up, but I kept a close eye on him as he stood. Zandra's magic slowly faded as she glared at him, clearly still irritated.

Habriel rubbed his throat, his wings twitching in agitation. "It's not my fault. I got the rules wrong, okay? I thought I could win by taking down the last prey standing."

"You should have paid more attention." Tempest crossed her arms. "This game isn't just about winning. It's about playing fair."

Habriel gave a small nod, still looking disgruntled. "Yeah, I get it. My bad."

I stepped back, allowing him to regain his composure, but ready to pounce if he tried anything else. The tension slowly eased as it became clear the fight was over.

"Hey! I know you." Tempest strode closer to Habriel. "You're that singer."

He flashed a dazzling smile, although there was no warmth in it. "You're a fan?"

Tempest frowned. "Your music isn't terrible. Your drummer's decent."

"High praise indeed," Habriel said.

Zandra was still looking at Tempest. "I don't get it. Why are you here so early? You're not supposed to be here until tomorrow night."

Wiggles mooched into view, chewing on something he shouldn't. "Surprise!"

"Wiggles thought it would be fun to show up early," Tempest said. "He remembered the Yuletide witch hunt was taking place today. And there was some hassle about decorations, so I needed a swift escape. You know how Granny Dottie gets about her tree."

"Oh. Sure. Well... I guess it's okay that you're here early," Zandra said. "I haven't sorted your bed out, though."

"I'll crash in with you. We've done it before."

"And I'll have your pillow," Wiggles said.

"Only if you don't snore," I said. "You may prefer the yard. The fresh air will help you sleep."

"We're not sleeping in the yard! Jeez, you two! What a frosty welcome." Tempest briefly hugged Zandra, which she returned. Neither of the witches were big on public displays of affection, so this embrace was the equivalent of being enveloped in a giant hug from a muffin-scented grandmother for five minutes.

"You're not dressed up properly," Habriel said to Tempest.

She glanced at him. "These ears don't belong to me."

"That's just a brown coat!"

Tempest glowered at him for daring to interrupt the family reunion. "What of it?"

"Since you've been quoting the rules at me, you have to be in a proper costume. Even if you're the last witch standing, you'll be eliminated because you broke the rules, too. That makes me the winner!"

"Tempest can break any rule she likes and get away with it," Wiggles said.

"Not this one," Habriel said. "I want that hamper."

"Why? You could buy a dozen of those things with all the money you must make from your music," Tempest said.

"He's really that famous?" I asked.

"I guess. If you're into that sort of thing," Tempest said.

"Millions of people are," Habriel said. "And I was in the top five most eligible angels in *Rockstar Magazine* this year."

Tempest and Zandra shared an amused look.

"Who got the top spot?" Zandra asked.

Habriel's dazzling smile faded. "I forget. And I'm freezing. Should we go back and see if I'm the winner?"

"You can't win," I said. "Only magic users with bonded familiars can win the hamper."

Habriel shrugged. "They'll make allowances for me. If I brought this witch down and she was the last magic user standing, then it's mine."

A scatter of brilliant red light lit the sky.

"Bad luck," I said. "That's the signal we have a winner. And it's not you."

Habriel pouted. "I didn't want the dumb hamper, anyway." He turned and strode off, not waiting for us.

"The angels around here are grumpy." Tempest fell into step with Zandra as we headed back toward the start.

"He's not one of ours," Zandra said. "He's just visiting."

"I found one of his friends, Nisroc, injured in the woods," I said. "Apparently, a friend shoved him over in the excitement. I had to heal his ankle."

"It was probably that jerk." Tempest gestured with her chin at Habriel. "These famous types are all the same. They get an over-inflated ego and think they can do what they like. It always leads to trouble."

"Trouble that means we lost the hamper," Zandra said.

"Vorana will feed us so much food over Christmas we won't be able to move," I said. "Although it would have been delicious to win that ham.

Perhaps Sage was victorious. She said she might share with us."

We trudged through the trees, cold and hungry, until we got back to the start of the hunt. Barney Hoffman and his familiar Ember Dreamscape had won the contest. It was a surprise, but a welcome one. Barney was a decent boss with a big heart, and although Ember could be annoying when he got overly excited, he was a solid familiar. While everyone crowded around and congratulated them, Nisroc walked over with Bertoli.

"Sorry you didn't win," Nisroc said to me. "That was my fault. You stopped to help me. You didn't need to do that."

"I won't ever leave an injured man behind," I said.

"I talked to Bertoli, and he said you can come to our party if you like," Nisroc said. "It's my way of saying thank you for helping me."

I looked up in surprise at Bertoli. "I heard the food will be excellent,"

He pursed his lips. "Of course. Free food and drink. We're having a party in the restored manor house tomorrow night. There'll be other angels there, but my alumni party will have a private area. You can't come in that section, but you can stop by for a short while."

I looked over at Zandra. She wrinkled her nose but nodded. "We'll be there."

"And we require a plus four," I said.

Bertoli paused. "Plus four?"

"For Tempest, Zandra's sister, and Tempest's familiar, Wiggles. And my Sammy and Randal Nix."

Zandra glowered at me. "There's no need to invite Randal to the party."

"They're all welcome, aren't they?" Nisroc asked Bertoli.

He shrugged. "Just don't cause trouble."

Tempest smirked at Zandra. "Who's Randal?"

"No one." Zandra shot me a baleful look.

"He's an adorable tech mage who's sweet on Zandra," I said. "I've been trying to get them together, but things keep getting in the way. We need Christmas magic to assist."

"We'll leave you to enjoy the evening. See you tomorrow at the party." Nisroc headed off with Bertoli.

Zandra tried to walk off, but Tempest grabbed her arm. "No, you don't. Who's this guy you're into?"

"Juno made a mistake," Zandra said. "How's your fallen angel?"

"Rhett's great, thanks. But we're not talking about my relationship." She slung an arm around Zandra's shoulder and pulled her in close. "Come on. You can tell me all about Randal over festive hot chocolate and brownies. And don't leave anything out. I'll know if you do."

I walked behind the witches with Wiggles, a cat smile on my face. It was time to let the festive celebrations continue.

# Chapter 3

## Party time

"I've never visited Willow Tree Falls, but I've heard plenty of rumors about it." Sorcha Creer set down a plate of frosted brownies and another of sugared doughnuts with tiny edible paper reindeer decorating the tops. "Breakfast treats for all!"

"What rumors would those be?" Tempest leaned back in her seat in the café and fixed a level stare on Sorcha.

Her eyes widened a fraction. "Oh, you know. The demon prison. Your family. I didn't mean any offense."

"Ignore her," Zandra said, as she helped herself to a brownie. "Tempest has never been a morning person. She's sometimes not even an afternoon person."

"Neither are you." Tempest grabbed her own brownie. "These look great. Thanks."

"You're welcome. I'm promoting festive specials for the rest of the month, and I heard a rumor you liked brownies, so I figured you'd appreciate these."

"You hear a lot of rumors, don't you?" Tempest asked. "Are you the gossipy sort? Have a problem keeping secrets?"

"If you keep being mean to my friends, you can find your own table to sit at," Zandra said. "Be nice or shove off."

"I'm always nice!" Tempest peered inside her leather jacket, which she had partially zipped. When we'd gotten back to Vorana's after the Yuletide witch hunt yesterday, she'd discovered I was still fostering the now not-so-tiny black kittens Sorcha had left in my care. Much to Wiggles' frustration, the kittens bonded with Tempest and had refused to leave her side, which was how they came to be tucked inside her leather jacket, fast asleep, settled against her belly.

"I need to get back to work. My customers love their festive brownies. Enjoy your breakfast." Sorcha dashed off, clearly eager to be away from Tempest's grouchy morning mood.

The café was busy, with residents out buying last-minute Christmas gifts and soaking up the cheery atmosphere, while grabbing a cream topped hot chocolate.

The main high street in Crimson Cove was festively decorated, and most of the stores had created cute window displays. The atmosphere was happily hectic as people bustled around, trying to get organized in time for Christmas.

The café door swung open, and Cythera marched in, heading for our table. From her angry glare, it was easy to assume she wouldn't be wishing us a seasonal salutation. She ignored us all except Tempest, who she speared with an icy stare.

"I got an alert you were in town," Cythera said.

"Greetings! Have you recovered from last night's woodland fun?" I asked. "The costume you wore was adorable."

Cythera ignored me. Her manners had gone downhill since she'd gotten high on all those weird mushrooms. "I'll only say this once. Behave while you're here. This is my town, and I maintain the peace."

Tempest munched on her brownie, her gaze straight ahead. "I'm just visiting family. And whatever you've heard about me isn't true."

Cythera loomed over Tempest. "I know you come with a troublesome demon. This is a peaceful town, and we don't need that kind of chaos."

"As much as it pains me to correct you, Tempest only has a tiny amount of demon inside her these days," I said. "She was good enough to share that problem with Zandra and their other sister, Aurora."

Tempest nodded. "Juno's got the facts right. You need to update your records."

Cythera fluttered her wings. "My records are always up to date. I've also spoken to my Willow Tree Falls colleague about you."

"I'm sure Dazielle sang my praises," Tempest said. "Although I'm interested to know when you last spoke to her?"

Cythera hesitated. "Recently."

"Last week?"

"No."

"Last month?"

"I don't recall. I've been busy."

"Busy getting your facts wrong. Dazielle is away on secondment, and my demon has been dealt with," Tempest said. "Thanks to my sisters' support, he'll never bother anybody again. Now, if you'll excuse us, we're having a family get-together, and the last time I checked the genealogy records, we had no angels in the bloodline. Move along."

Cythera's nostrils flared. "Your mutt is eating the town's ceremonial yule log! We're burning it tonight, and I don't want it smelling of sulfur and pee."

"I wondered where he'd gone." Tempest smirked. "Wiggles has developed this weird habit of chewing on wood. I think it's a stress reliever."

"Stop him! You won't get another warning." Cythera turned on her heel and stalked away.

"We'll see you later at the party," I called out.

Cythera turned back, her hand on the door. "What are you talking about?"

"We received a generous invitation to attend your exclusive gathering," I said. "I assume you're going. You got an invitation, didn't you? I know the party is for Bertoli and his alumni classmates, but surely, they wouldn't exclude such an esteemed and well-liked member of Angel Force."

Tempest openly chuckled, while Zandra hid a smile.

Cythera's brow furrowed. "If I see so much as one wrong move from any of you at that party, you're all out. One of you messes up, you all face the consequences." She yanked open the door and stomped off.

Tempest shoved the last of the brownie into her mouth. "She's fun."

Zandra shrugged. "Cythera's a lot less frosty than she used to be."

"We've thawed her out," I said. "She sometimes even grudgingly accepts our help when she's stuck on an investigation."

"These angels can be so uptight," Tempest said. "It took what felt like an eternity to get respect from the Willow Tree Falls angels. They looked at my surname, and that was it. I was labeled a demon peddling troublemaker with a chip on my shoulder."

"They were half right," Zandra said.

Tempest shoved her. "I have barely any demon left to bother me, and my chip is way smaller than it used to be. Let's take the rest of this food to go. I'd better grab Wiggles before he ruins your Yule log and the whole town turns against us."

We said a quick goodbye to Sorcha, who was serving iced gingerbread men to a group of children, and left the café. It had stopped snowing, but more loomed overhead as our feet and paws crunched through the fresh powder, heading to the center of town.

A huge fir tree had been erected and was covered in magical decorations that sparkled and twirled with a life of their own. In front of the tree was a giant log that had been cut in January and left to season for the year. Residents would gather around it at dusk to burn it, as was the tradition at Yule. Unfortunately, a large chunk had vanished from one end, and Wiggles was currently bouncing around on the top of it, his tail up.

"Get down!" Tempest said as we drew nearer. "I've just had Angel Force on my back because of you."

"I'm doing nothing wrong." Wiggles remained where he was. "And I'm a dog. We're supposed to chew sticks."

"You're a powerful hellhound who could destroy that thing with a gassy burp," Tempest said. "Off the Yule log, or no gifts for you. You don't want to spoil the celebrations for everybody else."

His ears drooped. "I was only having fun."

"I can show you plenty of places for fun," I said as Wiggles hopped off the Yule log and joined us. "And you might like to meet some of my friends. Archie is a full-sized hellhound, and he lives close by with a vampire hive. He's their protector. Well, they protect each other."

"He sounds cool," Wiggles said. "I like the ice sculptures. We should go look at them."

"Don't even blow smoke near them," Tempest warned him. "If you melt those sculptures, we'll get kicked out of town."

"I only want to look! And maybe pee on a few. It's fun to see the steam."

Tempest groaned as we headed to the sculptures set around the fir tree. All different supernaturals were represented, from angels to vampires. They'd been expertly carved, with each artist spending weeks ensuring the designs were perfect before they were installed.

"It's a nice town you've got here." Tempest stood with her hands on her hips. "Maybe we should consider a move here."

Zandra's mouth dropped open, and she shot me a horrified look.

Tempest burst into laughter. "Kidding. Why don't you show me around, though?"

I hopped onto Zandra's shoulder and leaned close to her ear. "Try not to panic. Families test us to the limits during the holidays."

Zandra scowled at Tempest's back as she strolled ahead of us with Wiggles beside her. "I hope we get through this test in one piece and all come out the other side alive!"

***

"You scrub up nice, sis." Tempest was lounging on Vorana's couch while she waited for us to get ready for the Angel Force party. She wore a smart, fitted black pantsuit with a sparkly sequin top underneath, also in black. Wiggles sat next to her, sporting a fetching sparkling bowtie, and had clearly had his fur brushed.

"Thanks. You look good, too. Is that outfit new?" Zandra asked.

"No, but you know what Granny Dottie is like. She insisted I pack something smart because she knew there'd be parties. She wouldn't let me leave the village until she'd inspected what I was bringing."

"She loves everyone to look bougee." Zandra wore a form-fitting dress I'd encouraged her to wear. It was a deep red with a daring back that revealed a lot of skin. She'd complained for several minutes before succumbing to my clothing demands. But there was a good reason I wanted her to look so fancy tonight.

As if on cue, there was a knock at the front door.

"I'll get it." I dashed away and flipped open the door with a practiced twist of my paws to reveal my sweet companion Sammy standing outside, looking magnificent. Beside him was a nervous-looking Randal Nix.

Randal tugged at his collar, his bowtie already crooked. He held a bouquet of winter flowers.

"Greetings. You're right on time. Everyone's ready to leave," I said.

"Am I dressed okay?" Randal asked. "I've never been to an Angel Force party before. I didn't know if I should wear all white. They love their white."

"You look divine." He wore a smart velvet suit with drainpipe pants and oversized lapels. It was as if he'd stepped out of the nineteen-seventies, but the look suited him.

"Come in. Zandra and Tempest are in the living room." I gently head-butted Sammy in greeting, and then we returned to gather the rest of the party.

Randal made a choking sound as he spotted Zandra. "Wow! You look great. Have I ever seen you in a dress?"

"Oh! I didn't realize..." She looked at me, and her eyes narrowed. "Of course. You're coming to the party."

"It's still alright, isn't it?" Randal glanced at me. "Juno said it was last minute, but you needed backup. You know I'm happy to back you up any day."

"So, this is the boyfriend, huh?" Tempest rolled off the couch.

"No, this is my friend," Zandra said, quickly making the introductions.

Randal seemed unable to keep still as he twitched and fidgeted under Tempest's fierce scrutiny.

"We'll talk later," Tempest said to him, her gaze never wavering from his face. "I need to know you're taking care of my little sister."

"I'm not a child," Zandra hissed at her.

Tempest pursed her lips, her steely gaze remaining on Randal. "Do you drink?"

"Now and again," Randal said. "But not often. It doesn't agree with me."

"Good. No one likes a sloppy drunk."

Wiggles sniffed around Randal, and for a second, I worried he might cock his leg. "He's got power. He might be a match for Zandra. You need to be able to keep up with these Crypt witches, buddy. They're not slouchy."

"Stop inspecting Randal like he's a piece of meat." Zandra gestured at the door. "And unless we want to be late, we need to leave."

Tempest stood to attention and saluted, a grin on her face. "Lead the way. They're your angels, and this is your town. I'm just here to have fun and make sure my little sister is behaving. But not too much."

Zandra rolled her eyes.

Everyone gathered their coats and put on winter boots before we headed outside into the freezing evening air. Snow was falling again, sparkling as it drifted around us.

Randal fell into step beside Zandra. "I heard there was a famous angel going to be at this party."

"You mean Habriel," I said. "We met him at the Yuletide witch hunt. Tempest recognized him. She's a fan of his music."

Tempest shrugged. "Hardly! I've seen a picture of him. I don't know the guy, and his music's not that great. It's generic pop-rock. The ladies seem to like him, though."

"He's handsome in a unique way," I said. "He looks like an angel, but he's got an edge."

"It sounds like you have a crush," Sammy said good-naturedly.

"I devote all my crushes to you," I said.

"Habriel's nothing special," Tempest said. "So, what's with this posh manor house we're partying in?"

"The place has been abandoned for a long time," Zandra said. "It was bought about eighteen months ago, and there have been workers going in and out ever since. It's not finished yet, but I guess whoever owns it offered it to Angel Force for their posh event."

"Perhaps it's another angel," I mused. "Whoever it is, they have a lot of money. I snooped around there once or twice when it was derelict. It would have been easier to pull it down and start again."

"Maybe we'll meet the mysterious owner tonight," Zandra said.

I cocked my head as a faint meowing reached my ears. I looked at the backpack Tempest had insisted on bringing instead of a more suitable purse for such a fancy event. "Have you brought those kittens with you?"

"I don't know what you're talking about."

"They're chaos makers! If they get loose at the party, Cythera will eat you alive."

Tempest smirked. "She can try. They started crying when I put them down for a nap, so what was I supposed to do?"

"Give them extra food and tuck them in for the night," I said. "They were never like that with me."

"Those kittens are obsessed with her," Wiggles grumbled. "And they hate me. They keep hissing every time I get too close. One of them even shot a fireball at me."

"I hope you shot one back," I said. "They may be babies, but they're full of power. I've yet to determine its source, but it's not to be messed with."

"They have too much power," Tempest said. "That's why I'm keeping watch over them. There's something different about these kittens, and I need to make sure they're not full of trouble."

"They're kittens!" Zandra said. "That's what they're made for. Adorable, fluffy trouble."

"They won't be a problem at the party," Tempest said. "There'll be a cloakroom where I can tuck them in. I'll use calming spells over them to chill them out. They're less frantic when they're with me, so it's the easier option. If I left them behind, they'd break out of the house, charge through the snow, and find some problems to get muddled in."

"Just make sure they don't burn down this newly spruced-up manor house," Zandra said, "or Cythera won't just be kicking you out of town. She'll do the same to us."

Tempest slung an arm around Zandra's shoulders. "Stop worrying and let's start partying."

# Chapter 4

## Angel groove

"How many of those have you had?" Cythera lurked close to Tempest, her gaze on the sugar-rimmed shot glass in her hand.

"Two lemon drops, and I'm done." Tempest tossed back the drink. "I know my limits. And I didn't come here to get wasted. My visit to Crimson Cove is long overdue, so I'm not wasting a second of it with a hangover."

"I'm watching you." Cythera pointed at her own eyes with two fingers and then jabbed them at Tempest.

"You can watch me all you like, but it'll be a waste of your time," Tempest said.

I jumped on the bar, placing myself firmly between the two powerful magic users who'd been bickering on and off for an hour. "This is a party, not a negotiation to stop a magical battle from erupting and spoiling Christmas. Cythera, go and entertain Maverick. He looks bored."

"My husband will never be bored. He can always find someone to talk to, even if they don't want his company."

"You go and be that someone," I said. "And stop picking on Tempest."

"Yeah, stop picking on me." Tempest lounged against the bar that had been installed in the grand dining room for the main party, a familiar smirk on her face, showing she was unfazed by Cythera's ominous lurking.

Cythera muttered under her breath as she marched away across the polished wooden floor.

"I'll have another round of smoky emerald shots, please." Nisroc, the angel I'd helped in the woods, set down an empty tray on the bar.

"Greetings!" I said to him.

He smiled, although it looked forced. "Hey! I'm glad you could make it."

"I'm happy to be here, and this is quite some party."

Nisroc glanced at the glittering decorations and extensive buffet that had turned the magnificent dining room into a sparkling winter wonderland full of tasty treats. "The angels aren't known for hosting lackluster events."

"I don't know about that," Tempest said. "I've been to a few stinkers."

I made the introductions before Tempest wandered off to see what Wiggles was getting up to and to check on the kittens.

"If I'm not mistaken, this is your fifth trip to the bar," I said to Nisroc. "I didn't know angels liked to drink so much."

He shrugged. "It's always been like this."

I glanced at his gaggle of raucous friends. The alumni class had their own private section, which was roped off so the rest of the angels and guests couldn't gatecrash their exclusive soiree. "You're acting more like a waiter than part of the group."

"Really? I... I hadn't noticed." Nisroc ducked his head. "I like to be useful."

"There's being useful, and then there's being taken advantage of. Why run around collecting drinks for everyone all evening? You're part of the group, too. Don't you want to relax and enjoy yourself?"

"Sure. Who doesn't? But we all have different roles we play, don't we?"

"I play the role of magnificent feline familiar to perfection," I said. "How would you describe your role?"

Nisroc hesitated. "I go along to get along. It's easier that way."

"Some may call that being a pushover."

"Maybe they do, but you need to figure out a way to get through this life without it being too tough."

"Tough? Is someone in particular making things tough on you?" I deplored bullies. Any kind of cruelty was unacceptable, whether it was toward a magic user or an animal. It didn't matter. The way you treated another person was a testament to your own character.

When Nisroc didn't respond, I pressed for more. "When I saw you in the woods yesterday, you said someone shoved you over. Was that shove an accident or deliberate?"

"Does it matter?"

"Of course it does. Give me the rogue's name, and I'll bring them to task," I said.

"I want no trouble. I help out the guys, and I keep my head down. That works for me."

I studied the group Nisroc was a part of. Habriel was once again leading the pack, flaring his wings and telling some tall tale as he flung his arms around. "It's easy to be overshadowed by someone as flamboyant as Habriel, especially with his level of fame."

"Some of us are born for that lifestyle," Nisroc said. "It would be my idea of hell on earth if you told me to get on a stage in front of thousands of screaming people and sing."

I kept my focus on Habriel. "Habriel's wings are an unusual color. I didn't notice the first time we met, but are those speckles in his wing feathers?"

Nisroc collected his drinks and turned. "It's all for show. The same with the eyes. He uses magic to darken them, so he stands out. And yeah, he dyes his wings. He calls it art."

"You don't sound convinced," I said.

"I've heard people say that anything can be art—from a broken brick to the most magnificent watercolor. So, if you use that definition, then Habriel is a walking work of art. He's sculpted himself into an image that endures. The attention makes him happy."

"And what do you think about it?"

He glanced at me. "Just between us?"

"You have my word."

"He's a poser."

There was a yelp, and something hit the floor. I turned to see Wiggles had upended a tray of treats from the buffet table and was scarfing them down. "If you'll excuse me. My friend appears to have forgotten his manners."

Nisroc nodded and walked off with his drinks, while I dashed in the other direction to prevent Wiggles from causing pandemonium.

"I'm glad you're here," he said the second I arrived. "Did you know there's a cheese fountain?"

"Stop gobbling those treats so quickly, or you'll get indigestion," I said. "Why should I care about a cheese fountain?"

"Are you insane? Cheese! It's one of the best foods."

"I enjoy a small amount as a pizza topping, but I'm a little intolerant," I said.

"It's at the other end of the buffet. Follow me." Wiggles bounded off before I could stop him.

I offered an apology to the wait staff as they tidied his mess then dashed after him. "You must behave! Cythera is on high alert, and she's looking for an excuse to kick us all out."

"She's nowhere to be seen." Wiggles circled the giant fountain of gooey cheese. The perimeter of the fountain had a shelf around it with bowls of treats that could be dipped into the cheese. It was a tempting sight. "I'm too short to get up there on my own."

"There's a reason for that. No one wants hellhound fur in the melted cheese," I said. "Where's Tempest? She can get you a bowl of cheese."

"I want to stick my head in and drink the lot."

"If you do that, you'll be violently ill."

"I have a cast-iron gut. I can eat anything. I once ate a rotting demon's finger."

My booping snooter wrinkled on its own. "Why do such a disgusting thing?"

"I thought it was a sausage. It had turned brown, and I had a head cold, so my sense of smell wasn't up to much."

He was such a revolting creature. "No cheese drinking! Not until Tempest comes back and can supervise your gluttony."

"I just need a boost up," Wiggles said. "Or maybe someone to act as lookout while I make a leap for it. If I add some magic to my bounce, I can make it. I know I can. I'm manifesting my success."

"No boosting, and no leaping. Come away from the cheese."

Wiggles huffed smoke in my face then dropped his head and trudged away from the cheese fountain. He turned, crouched, and leapt. His front paws met the edge of the fountain, and he kicked and scrambled until he was perched precariously on the rim.

"Get down from there," I hissed. "People are looking."

"They'll want to see this." Wiggles flipped onto his back, opened his mouth, and let the hot, gooey cheese pour into it. As more people saw him, there were gasps and murmurs of disapproval.

I jumped and grabbed hold of his stubby tail, attempting to yank him out of the fountain before he embarrassed himself. He gurgled but wouldn't budge. He was a stocky little fellow.

"Get out of that fountain before Cythera sees!" I dug my claws into his tail, and he growled.

With a powerful flick of his back feet, I found myself propelled through the air. I flipped, and as I came down to land, I realized with horror that my destination was the middle of the cheese fountain.

I howled in fury as my paws landed in the hot mess. I quickly sank. It was much deeper than I'd realized, and my head went under, causing me to inhale cheese. I swam to the surface, coughing and spluttering up melted cheese.

Wiggles looked over and gurgled happily, pleased to see me swimming about next to him.

"I knew it! I knew you wouldn't behave!" Cythera marched over, fury flickering in her eyes and her wings splayed wide. She grabbed us and yanked us out of the cheese, sending warm yellow goo splattering across the floor, causing guests to dodge out of the way so their fine outfits wouldn't be ruined.

"That was so worth it." Wiggles licked his muzzle, still being held at arm's length by a disgusted-looking Cythera.

"That's it. You two are out. And where are Zandra and Tempest? They should have been watching you, so they're out too," Cythera said.

"Hey! Get your hands off my hellhound." Tempest marched over with Zandra beside her.

"All of you are out of here." Cythera strode to the exit, still carrying Wiggles and me. She kicked open the door and slung us into the snow. She turned with a whirl of her wings and tossed Tempest and Zandra out, too. The door slammed in our faces.

I lay on my back, covered in stinky cheese that was rapidly cooling, humiliation burning through me.

Zandra leaned over me, her nose wrinkled. "What did you do?"

"Tried to save Wiggles from cheesemageddon. I shouldn't have bothered."

"I'm glad we got kicked out. It was a boring party," Tempest said. "Although Zandra was having fun flirting with Randal."

"There was no flirting!"

"I was enjoying myself until I ended up floating in hot cheese," I grumbled. "And I got to spend time with my Sammy. At least he didn't get tossed out, too."

"I was only there for one thing." Tempest twirled her fingers in the air and our coats and the kittens appeared in her arms.

"What was that?" Zandra attempted to pick frozen cheese out of my fur.

"The hamper, of course. It's being presented to the winners tonight, but I figured we deserved it more."

"You stole Barney and Ember's hamper?" I shook my head in disbelief.

"The angels will replace it with another one," Tempest said. "I stashed it out the back after checking on the fluffies. Let's grab it, get out of here, and enjoy a feast."

Zandra lifted me out of the snow. "First, a bath for you."

I didn't complain. I stank of cheese.

"But then we eat!" Tempest rubbed Wiggles down with a handful of snow.

"What's that saying about not being able to pick your family?" Zandra whispered to me.

"I heard that!" Tempest lobbed a cheesy snowball at her. "Stop griping and let's move. We have a stolen stash to enjoy."

I woke the next morning with a food hangover, an upset stomach, and a desperate need for fresh air. The cheese I'd inhaled had curdled inside me, and I'd topped it off with a few treats from the stolen hamper, so I was well and truly in trouble.

It took me fifteen minutes of cajoling and prodding before I got everyone else out of bed, up the stairs, and into the brisk, freezing morning air. Once outside, my head soon cleared, and my stomach felt less riotous. Tempest and Zandra trudged ahead through the snow, mugs of coffee in hand, while I lingered behind with Wiggles.

"I hope you're feeling sorry for yourself after last night's adventures," I said to him.

"I have no regrets. I live by the motto: I only regret the things I haven't done, not the things I have. And that was on my bucket list."

"Death by melted cheese?"

Wiggles laughed, and a plume of smoke billowed out around him. "You had fun, too."

"My stomach says otherwise," I said. "I thought becoming a father would have matured you."

"Cheese makes me do strange things." Wiggles smacked his lips together. "But I always make sure my pups are happy. You need to take care of the little ones. I set them a good example, and they're thriving."

"Let's hope the cheese story never gets back to them," I said.

"They've done much worse. What about those kittens, though? Are you planning on adopting them?"

"No. It's a long story, but Sorcha Creer, who runs the café, often fosters strays. We had a tricky few months in Crimson Cove, so I took over the role when she couldn't handle them."

"They're feisty, that's for sure," Wiggles said. "They'd give my pups a run for their money. And their power is zingy."

"I'm unsure what to do with them."

"As long as they don't come home with us, I don't mind," Wiggles said. "How's Zandra getting along these days?"

I glanced at my wonderful witch. "She has a sticky moment now and again, but she's adjusting well to being a sensible, employed adult with an intriguing, clever companion."

"You mean you?"

I swatted him with a paw. "Naturally."

"Zandra was full of chaos and anger when we first met," Wiggles said. "I wondered if I'd have to step in and deal with her."

"I'm glad you didn't," I said. "I've never had such a perfect bond."

"Yeah, these Crypt witches are something else," Wiggles said. "I was happy in my old life, just being a regular dog, mooching around, scratching myself, and eating all the treats I could con from people. But then I got magic, and boy oh boy, my life changed for the better."

"Zandra's magic has always felt different from Tempest's," I said.

"It's because she's got no Crypt witch blood. Don't get me wrong," Wiggles said, "she's part of our family through and through, but her dad and mom have different magic. She was trained to use the power the Crypt witches have, but she has no natural affinity with demons, does she? That's what makes the Crypt witches stand out."

"We've crossed a few demons since being here," I said. "Zandra never struggles to handle them."

"And she won't. There's something unique about her. It's a rare magic. And it's always shifting. It feels different."

"Sometimes, a miracle occurs, and it created my wonderful witch."

"My witch is more wonderful than yours," Wiggles said.

"Let's not put that to the test, shall we?" I said. "If the sisters go head-to-head, the town won't survive."

Wiggles chuckled. "Tempest would win."

"Zandra absolutely would." We stopped for a moment to admire the ice sculptures again, but were distracted by angels flying over our heads, and they were in a hurry.

"I figured the feathers would be sleeping it off after the party," Wiggles said.

"Let's see what's bothering them." They were flying straight to Angel Force, so I dashed after them and discovered a large group standing outside the building, including all of Bertoli's friends. Cythera had landed and was barking orders.

"What's got her knickers in a knot?" Wiggles asked. "I reckon it's about the hamper. Although would they get everyone together for one stolen hamper of goodies? They were amazing goodies. I ate all the chocolate tiffins, even though Tempest yelled at me not to."

"If you stop gabbing for a second, we'll find out." I clamped a paw against his muzzle to stop him from talking about food. This creature had a one-track mind.

"Maybe they haven't been stolen," an angel called out from the crowd.

"They were on display in front of all of us. Everyone at the party knew not to take them," Cythera said.

"Perhaps they've been borrowed?" another angel suggested.

"Or misplaced?"

There were grumblings among the crowd, and I wondered what they were talking about.

"Stop speculating! The books were on loan from the Academy," Cythera said. "We need all hands on deck to find them. Break into search parties and begin immediately."

"What's going on?" Zandra joined us, with Tempest beside her. "They can't be searching for the stolen hamper, can they? It's not that valuable."

"Something about missing books," I said.

Cythera saw us in the crowd, and after speaking to her angels for a few moments, she marched over. "Please don't say this is one of your tricks."

"We're guilty of nothing," I said. "But what's going on?"

"Was it you?" Cythera glared at Wiggles.

"All I was interested in last night was the cheese," he said. "And that mission was fully accomplished."

"What's this about missing books?" Zandra asked.

Cythera heaved out a sigh. "The Academy loaned us two first edition books. They were taken from the cabinet they were being displayed in at some point during the party. We must have them back. They're full of original Angel Force teachings. They're very important."

"Why would anyone steal something so boring?" Tempest asked.

"They may be boring to you, but there is angel power in those pages, and that cannot be misused."

"We're happy to help you search for the books in exchange for a free breakfast," I said. "I could enjoy another one of Sorcha's festive specials now my stomach has settled."

"Just get looking," Cythera snapped. "These books can't be lost."

By now, groups had split off, some flying back to the manor house, others intending to search the stores and streets in town.

Bertoli's friends were grouped together, although one of them was missing. That was when it struck me. When I'd stopped to look at the ice sculptures with Wiggles, there'd been a new addition to the collection. An angel who bore a remarkable similarity to Habriel.

I sped across the snow. "Bertoli, may I have a quiet word?"

"Not now, Juno. Cythera is tearing her hair out about the books, so we must find them."

"This is about the books! Follow me." I trotted back to the sculptures, and Wiggles, Zandra, and Tempest followed, along with Bertoli. "Does anything about this icy picture strike you as odd?"

He sighed. "I don't have time for this."

"Make time. It's important. Did Habriel commission an ice sculpture of himself to be put here?"

Bertoli shook his head. "Why would he do that?"

"Look again and let me know your thoughts."

Bertoli stared at the ice sculptures and gasped. He hurried over and touched Habriel's sculpture. He jumped back as magic sizzled off the ice. "Habriel has been frozen. And he's holding a book!"

Zandra scooped me up and set me on her shoulder. "Juno, this was supposed to be a quiet Christmas."

I watched Bertoli as he called for backup. "Maybe it still can be."

"Not with this new problem you've uncovered."

"We don't have to solve it if you don't want to."

She shook her head. "We will, won't we?"

"It wouldn't be Christmas without a little mystery to keep us entertained." And as I stared at the frozen angel clutching a book, my toe beans tingled. What a mystery this was!

# Chapter 5

## Popsicle

A group of shocked, tense angels surrounded Habriel's ice sculpture. When Bertoli realized what had happened, he yelled for his friends to join us, along with Cythera and several other angels.

I stood a short distance back with Zandra, Tempest, and Wiggles.

"He's not looking too good," Tempest murmured. "And I've seen something like this before. He's not getting out of there."

"I can feel the power coming out of that ice," Zandra said.

"Same here. And there's a reek to that magic. I don't like it." Tempest lifted her nose and inhaled deeply. "I smelled it when I first arrived in Crimson Cove."

"It's got to be something dark. No good spell would be able to do this to an angel," I said.

Cythera and her team fussed around the sculpture. She prodded at the ice, leaping back as a spark of magic shot out and burned her skin.

"I could try defrosting him," Wiggles said.

"He'd end up as a puddle in the snow," I said. "We don't need such drastic measures just yet."

We stood in silence as Cythera and Bertoli appeared stumped as they stared at Habriel.

"That must be one of the missing books he's got a hold of," Zandra said. "Maybe someone caught him stealing and taught him a lesson."

"Cythera said the books contained angel power, but Habriel's an angel, so he had access to all the magic he needed," I said.

"Perhaps he wanted access to spells he wasn't supposed to cast," Tempest said. "It wouldn't be the first time a good angel has turned bad."

I nodded in agreement. No supernatural was perfect. And despite what the angels said, they all had their flaws.

"A hellhound fireball will fix this." Wiggles was already trotting toward Habriel's frozen form, flames flickering out of his mouth. Habriel's friends saw him approaching and formed a circle, looks of horror on their faces as they flared their wings.

"Stand aside unless you want to get crispy," Wiggles warned, tipping back his head.

"Stop that creature!" Cythera yelled. "If he can't behave while he's in my town, he'll be locked in a cell."

That triggered Tempest, and she strode over to stand beside Wiggles. "Keep your uptight fingers off my hellhound. He's trying to help."

"By melting Habriel?" Bertoli shook his head. "He's frozen solid. If you use heat on him, it'll destroy him."

"I hate to break it to you." I joined Tempest and Wiggles while perched on Zandra's shoulder. "But Habriel is dead. That magic covering him is fatal. Perhaps if we'd discovered him the second it happened, we could have reversed the power."

"You don't know that for certain," Cythera said. "Unless, of course, you know what happened to him. Did you do this?"

"My dearest Cythera, the shock of finding an angel iced has clearly knocked logic from your brain," I replied. "Why would I freeze Habriel?"

"You were kicked out of the party," Cythera said. "You could be holding a grudge."

"So I killed a random angel I'd only just met? Think clearly. You threw us out, so I should have murdered you if a murderous desire had overtaken me. Which it didn't."

"Do you have an alibi?"

I glared at Cythera. Someone was prickly. "Do you know the time of death?"

She hesitated. "It must have been after the party ended. After midnight."

"That's simple. I was at home with these three while you all partied. I have no idea what Habriel was doing out here with one of your missing books. You have noticed the book clasped in his hand, haven't you? Is that one of the books you were looking for?"

"Of course I have." Cythera glowered at me then turned her attention back to the ice sculpture. She sighed. "When I touched the ice, I sensed no life there. But this makes no sense. Habriel was popular. He had adoring fans. Everybody liked him."

"Are you sure you don't want me to defrost him?" Wiggles asked. "Maybe you'll get a surprise and he won't melt."

Habriel's friends shuffled closer, their wings flared.

Wiggles shrugged. "If he's already dead, there's no harm in trying."

"You're powerful," Cythera said to Tempest. "You inspect the sculpture."

I grumbled into Zandra's ear, "Anyone would think Cythera had never met us. She knows we can solve any mystery."

"I'm happy to stay out of this. That way, we'll have minimal holiday stress."

Tempest glanced our way then headed to the sculpture. She lifted her hands and ran them down the ice, being careful not to touch it. "This dude is toast."

I observed Habriel's friends, who still stood guard, although they'd made space to allow Tempest to work. They appeared tense, but there were no tears. Could one of them be involved? Habriel appeared to be the life of the party and their group leader, but perhaps that had rubbed someone up the wrong way. Or they'd seen him with the book and confronted him. Habriel refused to give it back, and this was the result. But freezing him to death for theft was extreme.

"Angels, we need a search of the scene," Cythera said. "Look for evidence that points to who may have done this to Habriel."

Before she had a chance to group her angels into small search parties to check out the area, a tornado picked up a flurry of snow and whirled it toward us. The whirl of snow was blinding, and we all turned away and shut our eyes. When it died down, two higher angels had popped into view, showering us with snow and sparkles of light.

These otherworldly celestial beings oversaw Angel Force activities. They were so old and out of touch with real life that their rulings and behavior verged on the bizarre and ridiculous.

As I swiped snow off my whiskers with a paw, I was delighted to see my former nemesis, Tinkerbell, was with the angels. And I'd met these angels before. Bilious and Ted.

I jumped off Zandra's shoulder and trotted over. "Greetings! Were we expecting you in Crimson Cove for the holidays?"

"This isn't your business." Cythera flapped a wing at me.

I ignored her. Tinkerbell looked magnificent. Her black fur was glossy, and her eyes gleamed. She'd clearly taken well to life with the higher angels.

She flicked her tail up at me. "Juno! It's been too long. Well, I actually have no idea how much time has passed. The higher angels compress and expand time at will. It's amazing. You think you've been somewhere for a day, and only ten minutes have passed."

"That sounds fascinating," I said. "Bilious, Ted. Welcome back to Crimson Cove."

They bowed a greeting, both in flowing robes with shiny blond hair.

"Fascinating but not relevant." Cythera greeted the higher angels. "You're always welcome in Crimson Cove, but I didn't have your visit scheduled on my calendar. Is there a problem?"

"Visits must sometimes be unscheduled when a terrible tragedy occurs." Bilious rested a hand on Tinkerbell's plump side as he looked at the ice sculpture of Habriel and flinched. "This is a shame. We often listen to his music when we travel."

"I'm surprised you appreciate such modern tunes," I said.

"It's better than the classical dross this one likes." Bilious inclined his head toward Ted.

"Classical music is never dross. It's an acquired taste."

"It's dross," Bilious stage whispered.

"We've just discovered what happened to Habriel," Cythera said. "I was arranging search parties to see if any evidence had been left behind."

"There was snow coming down most of last night," I said. "Any clues would have vanished. And looking at Habriel's expression, it doesn't look like he put up a fight. If anything, he looks surprised, as if someone caught him unawares with a freeze spell."

"Thank you for your uninformed opinion." Cythera nudged me away with the toe of her boot. "I have everything under control. Go back to your witch."

"Alas, I fear you don't." There was a mournful expression on Ted's face. "When we received an alert that a prominent member of our Academy had perished, we had to intervene."

Bilious nodded. "Although Habriel didn't choose the path of law enforcement for long, he is still one of ours. And he died attending an alumni event organized through the Academy."

"That's all true." There was a note of caution in Cythera's voice. "But I'm still unsure as to why you're here. I have a successful track record of solving murders. You have nothing to concern yourself with."

"Angel Force is too close to this investigation," Bilious said. "It would be impossible for you to remain neutral if another angel was involved in this tragedy."

"I assure you, no angel under my charge would act so cruelly."

"Are you willing to bet your halo on that?" I asked.

Cythera drew in a breath and slid a glare my way. "We always act professionally. If Habriel's attacker was an angel, which I find highly unlikely, it won't be an issue. I will remain objective."

"Of course you will." Ted patted Cythera's arm. "But everything must be done by the book. The last thing we need is another scandal."

"You've had a recent scandal?" I asked.

"That isn't your concern," Cythera snapped.

"The wonderful Tinkerbell discovered it," Bilious said. "There was an internal investigation involving corruption in the permit and licensing department. Everything seemed aboveboard, and we were about to close the case when Tinkerbell found documents that revealed the sordid truth."

I twitched my whiskers. "And what was the sordid truth?"

"Nearly every angel in the department was rotten," Tinkerbell said. "They were taking bribes to hand out permits, no matter what they were for."

"Yes, it was a dreadful situation. Embarrassing, too," Bilious said. "And it caused a stir in our community. Angels are full of goodness and kindness, so I'm sure it was a misunderstanding, but we must be extra careful when there is any sniff of corruption or trouble. And, as you can imagine, an angel being murdered is a cause for concern."

"And odd," Bilious said. "We are immensely difficult to destroy. An angel has the power and strength to kill another angel, but why would they?"

Habriel's friends shuffled around, none of them looking happy at the possibility the finger of blame would be pointed at one of them.

I stepped forward and cleared my throat. "If I may—"

"Which is why we visited today, to most humbly request Tempest Crypt and her small, strange-smelling dog lead the investigation." Bilious beamed a radiant smile at Tempest.

I choked on my words. They didn't want us involved? I looked back at Zandra, and she shrugged, although she didn't look impressed at being passed over for her older sister.

"Please, Tempest, we would be most humbled if you would inspect the situation and give us your expert opinion." Ted gestured at Habriel. "What do you think happened?"

Cythera looked on with unmasked shock and disapproval.

Tempest snitched her nose and inspected the ice sculpture one more time. I could see she was trying not to laugh. "This isn't my town. And I'm on vacation. I'm not here to solve a crime."

"But you're a highly experienced investigator," Bilious said. "The best in the business."

Cythera fluffed out her wings, a scowl on her face. I felt as unhappy as she looked. Did everything we'd done to protect Crimson Cove mean nothing to these angels?

"Don't take it personally," Tinkerbell muttered to me. "You know what they're like. I love my angels, but I'm sure they screw their heads on the wrong way some mornings. Tempest's reputation is legendary among them. They share stories about her. It's like cult worship of the Crypt witches at some gatherings."

I tried not to stay annoyed, but it still stung.

Tempest stepped back and shook her head. "We pass."

Ted and Bilious gasped.

"What will we do if you don't assist us?" Ted asked.

"You have two experienced investigators already living in this town." Tempest pointed at us. "I don't know how Crimson Cove works. And I'm more into demons than angels, anyway. You'll get better results working with Zandra and Juno."

The higher angels consulted with each other for several minutes, leaving us waiting and getting thoroughly chilled in the snow.

I returned to Zandra and hopped onto her shoulder. "When they finally make the right decision, we should refuse to help. What a humiliation!"

"We can refuse if you like," Zandra replied. "I was planning on a quiet holiday, hanging out with friends and family, not figuring out who froze the singing angel with the stolen book. It sounds messy."

I studied Habriel's ice sculpture, his friends still surrounding him. "In the spirit of Christmas, I suppose we must help solve this crime."

Zandra huffed out a laugh. "You can never ignore a puzzle."

"Neither can you."

"Like you'd give me the option." Zandra leaned her head against my side. "I'm not missing out on hot chocolate and festive treats, though. We'll make time to have fun."

"We absolutely will." We'd solve this case swiftly to ensure we could enjoy ourselves without murder, suspects, and clues on our minds.

The higher angels finally stopped conversing. Tinkerbell leaped onto Bilious's shoulder and curled herself around his neck.

"It is agreed," Bilious said. "We have consulted our memories and accessed remote records. Although Zandra and Juno have less experience than Tempest and the small smelly beast, they are suitable replacements for this investigation."

I was tempted to lose my Christmas spirit and tell them where they could stick their investigation.

Cythera looked equally unimpressed by the decision. "I insist on being kept informed, though. I understand why you want the local branch of Angel

Force to take a step back, but this murder happened in my town, and I need to ensure people are safe."

"You can sort out the fine details with your associates," Bilious said. "Make a plan with Juno and Zandra and give them all the resources they request."

"And that includes a free breakfast every morning," I said. "You can't successfully solve a crime on an empty stomach."

Cythera flapped a wing at me in frustrated acknowledgment.

Bilious clapped his hands together and rubbed them briskly. "Now everything is sorted, it's time for our sleigh ride. On real reindeer in Lapland! We're so excited. Fairwell, my sweet simple beings." Another tornado of snow sparkles whipped the higher angels and Tinkerbell into it. I briefly saw Tinkerbell raise a paw in goodbye, and then they were gone in a flurry of freezing snow.

Tempest and Wiggles walked over and joined us, shaking snow off themselves.

"You don't mind that I lumbered you with the murder investigation?" Tempest asked. "I'm not in the mood for messing with higher angels. Or any angel, in fact. Especially not the one in charge, currently giving us death stares. Cythera has a serious problem with me."

"As you said, you're on holiday," I said. "Why would you want to spoil that with an icy crime?"

"And it's your town," Tempest added. "So, it's your business. I'm not here to solve a murder. I'm here to kick back and relax."

"And eat!" Wiggles said. "I'm starving. Is it time for second breakfast yet?"

While Wiggles discussed what he was going to eat, Zandra walked over to Habriel's ice sculpture, and we spent a moment looking at him. "So, where do we begin?"

I wrapped my tail around her throat to keep her warm. "We need to move this sculpture somewhere safe, and then we have a bunch of nervous angels to interrogate."

# Chapter 6

## Deep freeze

After Cythera and Bertoli had left the crime scene, along with Habriel's friends, we spent a few minutes looking around, but as expected, if there'd been evidence to reveal who'd frozen Habriel, it was obliterated by the snow.

"Ouch! Behave." Tempest peered inside her leather jacket.

"You're still carrying those kittens around?" I asked.

"They howl if I leave them alone. And they are kind of cute."

"You'll have to figure out something before you leave town," I said. "Although you're welcome to take them back to Willow Tree Falls. You mentioned how powerful they are, so they'll fit right in with the rest of the family."

"No way! Tempest only has one furry friend, and that's me," Wiggles said.

"You're good, buddy." Tempest zipped her jacket up and gently patted the wriggling contents. "We don't have room for this lot, especially not with your pups still bounding around out of control most of the time."

"I have them under control for at least twenty percent of the day," Wiggles said. "That's progress."

"It's freezing out here." Zandra stamped her feet. "We need to move Habriel so we can study him with no distractions. My toes are so cold I can barely concentrate."

"This calls for a visit to Sorcha's café," I said.

"I'm all for a visit to somewhere that serves such amazing food, but Habriel will melt if you put him inside," Wiggles said.

"Not if we translocate him into Sorcha's deep freeze," I said. "She's got a huge walk-in freezer at the back of the café, so he'll fit inside with no trouble."

"Don't you have a morgue?" Tempest asked.

"We do, but if memory serves, there's only a chest freezer, so we'd have to break Habriel into bits to fit him inside."

No one liked that idea, so after gathering around Habriel, I chose to translocate him and Zandra directly into Sorcha's deep freeze. Tempest and Wiggles decided to have their second breakfast and do some Christmas shopping, so we left them to it.

A second later, we arrived inside a frosty, misty freezer, surrounded by neat stacks of food. The door to the deep freeze opened, and Sorcha shrieked before slamming it shut again.

"Ah! We should have sent a message warning her of our arrival," I said. "But I could see the end of your nose was turning blue, so we had to hurry."

Zandra knocked on the inside of the door. "It's only us. We had an emergency delivery to make."

Sorcha inched open the door and peered in with wide eyes. "Is that the frozen angel everyone's talking about?"

"It is. We'd welcome the chance to get out of here before frostbite sets in," I said.

"Oh! Sorry. You startled me." Sorcha backed up and opened the door wider, allowing us out. "I was preparing food when I heard a thud and thought something must have fallen off a shelf. I never expected this!"

"We needed to store Habriel somewhere safe where he wouldn't defrost." Zandra rubbed her hands together to get the feeling back in them.

Sorcha wrinkled her nose. "I'm not comfortable having a frozen body in with food. It's unhygienic."

"I assure you, Habriel is made of ice. The spell used on him turned him into a complete ice sculpture, even the book he's holding. If he melts, he'll turn into a puddle of water. Your food will remain untainted by the dead angel," I said.

"That's still gross, but kind of fascinating," Sorcha said. "He can stay here for now. But if I get a surprise visit from the health inspector, you're explaining this weirdly gross situation."

"Heard and understood," I said. "We need five minutes to warm up, then we'll take a good look at him and make sure there's nothing toxic about his person."

"Juno's kidding about the toxic bit," Zandra said. "Hopefully."

Sorcha arched an eyebrow. "Good to know. And by warming up, I suppose you mean you need feeding?"

"Naturally. And we knew you wouldn't let us down. We're so cold." I gave a pitiful meow.

Sorcha chuckled. "Give me five minutes with the customers. Help yourselves to whatever is out here. And then I want to hear everything."

While Sorcha served at the café counter, we snooped around the kitchen and were soon happily settled. Zandra had a large coffee, hot chocolate with cream on top, and a festive sandwich of pigs in blankets and stuffing. I opted for a plate of pigs in blankets and a side order of grilled bacon.

Sorcha returned, wiping her hands on a clean cloth. "The rumors are already spreading that there was an extra ice sculpture discovered this morning. And now, he's in my freezer!"

"It was an angel visiting for the Angel Force alumni party," Zandra said. "Habriel was one of Bertoli's friends. They went to the Academy together."

"And he was famous," I added. "I didn't recognize him, but he was a singer in a band."

"Habriel?" Sorcha's eyes widened. "You don't mean the singer from Starlight Wings, do you?"

"Beats me," Zandra said. "I didn't recognize the guy, either."

Sorcha was just opening the freezer door to take another look when Vorana and Sage poked their heads into the kitchen.

"I thought I heard voices back here. Do you mind if we join you? Everyone's talking about what's going on," Vorana said. "And I knew Juno would be in the middle of it all."

"The more, the merrier," I said. "I can recommend the pigs in blankets."

"Take a look at this!" Sorcha gestured Vorana over, and they peered into the deep freeze.

"Isn't that Habriel from Starlight Wings?" Vorana asked. "He's the dead guy? I didn't know someone famous had been frozen."

"Since you know him so well," I said, "were there any public feuds between him and any other stars that led to this frosty outcome?"

They stared at Habriel before backing out, and Sorcha secured the freezer door. "Habriel was the golden boy of pop-rock. His performances were mesmerizing."

"I can't think of any public spats he had with another singer," Vorana said.

I chewed on a piece of bacon. "So if he was known as the good guy of pop-rock, perhaps someone close to him did this? Someone from his alumni party?"

"Another angel? What does Cythera think about that idea?" Sorcha asked.

"We can't take her opinion into consideration. She's unable to remain impartial." I failed not to smirk.

Vorana barked a laugh. "Oh, wait. Are you in charge of this investigation?"

"We had no choice but to step up," I said. "The higher angels showed up in a sparkling flurry and insisted Cythera take a step back because she was too close to the case."

"She'll hate you taking over," Vorana said.

"No more than usual. And Cythera grudgingly accepted it was the most logical course of action," I said. "The higher angels were right. She was deflecting the possibility that an angel could be involved even before the evidence was gathered."

"I can understand why she'd do that. Angels are supposed to be the good supernaturals," Sorcha said. "The pinnacle of perfection."

"Maybe not this time. Now I can feel my toes, let's take another look." Zandra brushed off her hands, and we all returned to the deep freeze and stared at Habriel some more.

I stalked around the body, hopping lightly so my toe beans didn't freeze. "There are no signs of injury. I suppose they could have been filled in with ice."

"Habriel doesn't look angry or as if he was fighting," Sorcha observed.

Vorana nodded. "He looks perplexed."

"For that spell to have worked, whoever cast it would have needed to catch him off guard, or he would have fought back," Zandra said.

"Or it was someone he knew, so they were able to get close before throwing out the spell," I said. "Someone he knew and someone immensely powerful."

"Do you really think another angel would do this?" Sorcha asked. "You get the occasional shade of gray on an angel, but murder goes against everything they stand for."

"We have powerful magic users living in town who could pull off this spell," I said, "but what motive would they have for killing Habriel? As you said yourself, he was the golden angel of music. If everyone adored him, there's no reason for them to want him dead."

"Fans can get obsessive," Zandra said. "Did anyone notice stalkers or groupies lurking about after the angels arrived?"

"I saw no one lurking around the party when we got there," I said.

"I once went through that obsessive phase with the boy band Blackberry Orange. I had a thing about guys wearing eyeliner and skinny jeans." Vorana laughed. "I had all their posters and used to dream that, one day, one of them would marry me. I didn't mind which one. They were all so cute."

"I was the same," Sorcha said. "Although I liked long-haired rockers and guys who painted their nails black and thought about death too much."

"I had a fondness for a lute player once," I said. "The way he wore his pantaloons left nothing to the imagination."

"Lute player?" Zandra asked. "Are we talking Middle Age England?"

"It was niche music. A fad. Moving on," I said, "we have to question Habriel's friends. They were all at the party last night, so someone must have seen what happened. At the very least, they'd have seen when Habriel left."

"Does anyone know when he was frozen?" Sorcha shut the deep freeze, and we returned to finish the extra food she'd placed on the table. Mini chocolate fruity puddings with a hot chocolate sauce.

"Sadly for us, we were kicked out of the party before things got going," I said. "There was an unfortunate incident with a cheese fountain."

"And despite washing you, I can still smell cheese," Zandra said.

I discreetly sniffed my fur and grimaced. "I'll have another bath tonight. We'll go back to Angel Force and arrange to interview Habriel's friends. We need a pattern of his movements. And there may have been disagreements at the party we missed, and that will point us toward an obvious suspect."

"Before you go, you must try these." Sorcha pulled out a tray of warm apple pie bakes with crusted cinnamon sugar, and we spent ten minutes overindulging in the gooey delights, although Sage and I exchanged cake for fish sticks.

Once we were warmed through and had full bellies, we left the café and headed back into the biting cold. I spotted Tempest and Wiggles doing Christmas shopping, so rather than disturbing them, we left them to it and headed to Angel Force.

"I like Tempest," I said to Zandra. "It's a pity she doesn't visit more often."

"She has mellowed," Zandra said. "It must be an age thing."

"It's a happy thing," I said. "She's content. She got her happy ending with Rhett. Her business is a success, and the demon prison is stable. What more could a witch want?"

"I guess. She is less spiky."

I chuckled. "I expect she says the same thing about you. When we first met, you were pricklier than a giant cactus that had mated with a thorn bush."

"I wasn't that bad!" She grinned. "Although I had my moments. But you were wildly crazy, too."

"Then we found each other, and purrfection ensued," I said. "Even Wiggles seems mildly less stinky."

"You get used to the odor," Zandra said. "You go nose blind."

"He's adulting. That's the difference. He was talking about bringing his pups here."

Zandra groaned. "Have you forgotten what chaos they cause?"

"They could spend time with our kittens."

She glanced at me. "We don't have kittens."

"About that—"

"No! I'd rather solve a dozen angel murders under Cythera's evil glare than foster three out-of-control, powerful kittens. I want a quiet life, and that would be the opposite of quiet."

"They're fond of Tempest. I'll convince Wiggles they deserve a life of demonic fun in Willow Tree Falls."

"You work on that. But right now, we need to grill some angels."

We arrived at Angel Force, and I was delighted to see Habriel's friends were there, so it would be simple to question them.

"I don't want Cythera to think I'm stirring trouble," I murmured to Zandra, "but we should start with Bertoli. I consider him a friend, but he was at the party, and he's known Habriel as long as the others."

"I have no problem with that," Zandra said. "If only to eliminate him."

"Who's been eliminated?" Cythera marched over, obviously still chafing at not being given the task of leading this investigation.

"I prefer obliteration to elimination," I said, "and we were talking about suspects rather than the literal form of destruction."

"Then literally get on with it," she snapped.

"That's why we're here. And we'd like to start with Bertoli," I said.

Her eyes bulged. "Tell me that's the most unfunny joke you've ever told."

"We're serious," Zandra said. "We need to figure out what happened last night. Bertoli was friends with Habriel. He's got to be on the suspect list."

"It's okay." Bertoli had overheard the conversation as he hurried over. "I want to help. I've known Habriel a long time, and I want to get to the bottom of this as much as everyone else."

"It's wonderful to have such an obliging angel on hand." I looked pointedly at Cythera. "Let's take this into an interview room, shall we?"

"I'm coming too." Cythera followed us. "I'm Bertoli's legal representation."

"We know that's untrue," I said, "but you're welcome to sit in if Bertoli has no objection."

"It's fine," Bertoli said. "I don't mind. I've got no secrets."

We settled into the room, with Cythera and Bertoli on one side of the table and Zandra and me on the other.

"Let's keep it informal for now," I said. "Obviously, we know who you are, but can you tell us more about your connection to Habriel?"

"You already know that," Cythera said.

"We want to get the facts in order." Cythera was being unpleasantly prickly again. "Bertoli?"

"I met Habriel at the Academy," he said. "We were in the same cadet class together. We sometimes sat next to each other. And we shared a dorm room."

"Describe your relationship."

"Bertoli is a professional, and he was an outstanding student at the Academy," Cythera said.

"A fact, I have no doubt," I said, "but if you don't stop interrupting, I'll have to ask you to leave."

"This is my station! Bertoli is in my troop."

"And this is our investigation," Zandra said. "Shut it or get out."

Bertoli looked startled, while Cythera fumed silently.

"Please, continue," I said to Bertoli.

"I met Habriel on my first day. I got the impression he had big plans from the get go," Bertoli said. "He did well in his studies, but his passion was always music. We had an Academy choir, which he joined, and he was always talking about it. He arranged concerts and charity performances and was usually the lead singer."

"Did he go on to serve in Angel Force for long?" I asked.

"Two years," Bertoli said. "But he always kept singing as a sideline. Then he got discovered, and the rest is history. He joined his band, and less than a year later, they had their first hit single."

"How did you feel about his success?"

"I was happy for him," Bertoli said. "Why wouldn't I be happy for my friend? Habriel got to follow his dream and made it a success."

"You had no ambitions to become famous yourself?"

A resigned smile slid across Bertoli's face. "I know where my strengths lie, and it's not in playing up to an audience. This job suits me. I enjoy being methodical and organized."

"That does sound like you," I said.

"We know you were at the alumni party last night," Zandra said. "Did you spend much time with Habriel?"

"I dropped in and out of the group," Bertoli said. "Habriel was great fun, but he could be a bit..."

"Over the top?" I asked. "When I saw him, he was enjoying being the center of attention. Was that typical of him?"

"Sure. I was used to that," Bertoli said. "You know me. I'm not into wild parties. I'd spend half an hour with the group then walk around the room and go back again."

"Did you leave the party at any point?" I asked.

"No. None of us did. We were all there for the whole night."

"What about Habriel?"

"Him too," Bertoli said. "The party ended at midnight, and I walked home. The rest of the angels are staying at the Sleepy Stardust Sanctuary. Although not Habriel. He rented a private house. He said it was because he was a night owl and didn't want to keep everyone up. He likes to sing late at night. He did that when we were at the Academy. It used to drive some of us mad."

"Tell us exactly when you last saw him," I said.

"I suppose, by the time we finished saying our goodbyes and had a snowball fight on the way out, I last saw him around twelve fifteen in the morning. I headed home, the rest of the group went back to the hotel, and Habriel walked off to his rental."

"Alone?"

"Yes."

"Which direction did he head?"

"Through town. He walked straight past the ice sculptures," Bertoli said. "That must have been when he was caught. Unless he went back later. I don't know why he'd do that, though."

"Did you notice if he had one of the stolen books with him when he left the party?" I asked.

"Huh? Actually, no. Although he had a big coat, so I suppose it could have been under that."

"Why would he take your books?" Zandra asked.

"I couldn't tell you," Bertoli said. "I suppose only Habriel has the answer, so we may never know. It was most likely a joke. He was big on jokes."

"When Habriel went off alone at the end of the night, you didn't see anyone following him?"

"Bertoli would have told you that if he had," Cythera said. "This is a waste of my time and his."

I glanced up at Zandra, and we shared a nod. "Thank you for your time, Bertoli. You've been most helpful."

"Do we have your permission to leave?" Cythera was already shoving back her seat.

"You do. Send in the next victim, please," I said. "And some of that chocolate yule log I saw on a desk for Zandra. Questioning dangerous types always makes us hungry."

That comment earned me a tut and a fierce glare before Cythera left.

Bertoli lingered a second longer. "She's just tense. It's Christmas. It makes her grumpy."

"Grumpier than you, and we just questioned you about a dead friend," I said.

Bertoli sighed. "Habriel always wanted to go out in a blaze of glory."

"Well, he got an icy whimper," I said. "And we need to figure out why."

# Chapter 7
# Getting cold

Virgil was our next interviewee. After Zandra ate some of the delicious yule log kindly brought in by Bertoli, Virgil settled in front of us, a serene look on his classically handsome face. He had a square jaw, kind eyes, and neatly cut, polished fingernails. His smile was benign as he waited for the interview to begin.

"We're sorry for your loss," I began. "I understand you and Habriel had been friends for many years."

"Yes, these are sad times," Virgil said. "We all met at the Academy, and you know what starry-eyed youngsters are like. We were given the same dormitory for the first two years and promised each other we'd join the same Angel Force troop and never be apart."

"That didn't happen?" I asked. "Habriel didn't take to working in law enforcement?"

Virgil twirled his fingers, and snowflakes drifted through the air. "We all have our interests and specialties. Habriel's was music. Even when we were learning law enforcement codes, he'd hum a tune under his breath."

"What's your specialty?" Zandra asked.

"I still work for Angel Force," Virgil said. "I got my first posting straight after graduation. I've moved around a few times and jumped up the ranks somewhat, but I'm not hugely ambitious. I wouldn't like to run my own branch, for example. I'm content to take orders and follow them. I enjoy peace rather than the stress that comes with managing a troop of angels."

"Especially when they're not on their best behavior," I said.

Laughter danced in Virgil's eyes. "We all have our moments when we're not at our best. Stress often brings out the worst in people."

Zandra pointed a finger at the small pile of melting snow Virgil had materialized. "Is that where your focus is? Celestial magic?"

"Well observed. Yes, I study it in my spare time."

Zandra's eyes narrowed. "Including how to perfect the use of ice and cold?"

He hesitated, although his expression remained calm. "Naturally. Celestial magic has a connection to the elements. Everything is made up of celestial components. Whether we're talking about the tiniest speck of sand on a beach or the biggest stars shining in the solar system. It's a vast and complicated field of magic and would take an eternity to finesse it, so I focus on what I most enjoy."

"Cold and ice?"

Virgil nodded. "And snow. It's so beautiful."

"You can see where my wonderful witch is going with this line of questioning," I said. "You have a degree of control over the powerful elements of ice and snow, and Habriel was frozen to death."

"All of that is true, but if I'd committed such a heinous crime, would I have revealed my gift to you?" Virgil twirled his fingers again, and a small, perfectly formed snow cat appeared on the desk, bearing a remarkable likeness to myself.

"Some magic can't be held in," Zandra said. "And celestial magic is known to overtake the user. It turns them into a vessel, so they have little ability to control themselves."

"And if I were an average magic user with average skills, I would agree that was a problem," Virgil said. "But I am an angel."

He said the last sentence as if it needed no more explanation. Was it arrogance or confidence talking? The snow cat he'd made was lovely, so Virgil knew how to control this primal power.

"And you're forgetting," he continued, "I'm a member of Angel Force. We promise to protect and serve, not destroy and ruin lives. There'll be many who are devastated by what happened to Habriel."

"His family?" I asked.

"I know nothing about his family."

"Why not?"

"He didn't talk about them. There were rumors they served in the Great Angel War during the Clandestiny Period, but Habriel never confirmed it. It was as if they never existed. It's possible they died during that war, so it was too painful to talk about."

"What about his fan base?" I asked.

"Yes, that was who I was thinking about. They will be shocked. I haven't followed Habriel's career, but I heard from the others how famous he'd become with his band."

"That suggests you didn't stay close friends with Habriel after you both left the Academy," I said.

"Not as close as I am with some of the others," Virgil said. "All of us went into Angel Force, so there were more opportunities to meet at conferences or at training events. Habriel was there at the beginning, but his head had already turned toward music, and he was simply going through the motions before he could set himself free. When he began along that path, I found we had little in common. It happens with some friendships. They naturally drift."

"That was the only reason you were no longer friendly?" I asked.

"We were never unfriendly with each other," Virgil said. "We shared a history. People make long-lasting friendships during education. It's similar to a sibling bond. You share a unique experience of growth and development that no one else can ever understand. That's what kept us together."

"If you were friends with Habriel, why didn't you celebrate his success in the music business?" I asked.

"I didn't say there was no celebration, but music has little effect on me. I see how some are entirely absorbed by it, possessed by it, but I prefer the quiet. Perhaps it's because of my own interests. Celestial magic takes an immense amount of concentration to perfect." He twirled his fingers, and a small, pointed witch's hat appeared on the desk, a flurry of snowflakes swirling around it.

"Cute. Are you as good with ice as you are snow?" Zandra asked.

"They're similar elements, so yes. But as I've already said, I do no harm with my magic. I'm an angel and loyal to my profession." He lifted one shoulder. "Besides, I had no issue with Habriel. And I hadn't spoken to him for years. I can't remember the last time we had contact. He missed several recent events due to work commitments, and I've been busy forging my path in Angel Force and enjoying life."

As Virgil continued to revel in his passion for celestial magic, I got no sense he was concealing anything. He seemed single-minded in his interest, but revealing it to us had been risky. That skill placed him at the top of the suspect list. Since Virgil could control ice magic, he had the ability to freeze Habriel.

"Did you see Habriel leave the party at any point during the evening?" Zandra asked.

"No. From what I remember, he was there the whole time. The same as all of us. We all left together, just after the party ended at midnight. I'm staying in the Sleepy Stardust Sanctuary with the others."

"But not Habriel?" I asked.

"He liked his personal space, so he hired a house. I'm not sure where it is. It can't be far from the manor house because he chose to walk through the snow."

"What about the stolen angel books?" I asked. "Did Habriel pay them attention during the party?"

"Even though they were on display for all to enjoy, I don't think he so much as glanced at them," Virgil said. "But then, we weren't joined at the hip. I suppose he could have taken a look."

"Why would he bother to take them if angel law held no interest?"

Virgil hesitated again, and snow fell onto his wings. "Habriel was fun to be around, but he was occasionally impulsive. He acted before he thought. Maybe he believed it would be funny to take the books and pretend they were lost."

"But then he was caught red-handed and frozen to death," I said. "Would taking the books be a motive for someone wanting Habriel dead?"

Virgil's eyes widened. "I find that unlikely. There is power among those pages, but nothing that would benefit Habriel. Taking the books would have been an embarrassment to Cythera and Bertoli, but nothing more. The books aren't the reason he died."

"What is the reason?" I asked.

"I couldn't tell you. I'm really sorry that I sound unhelpful, and I don't mean to be, but I'm unable to figure out why anyone would want to end an angel's life."

"Did you leave the party at any point?" Zandra asked.

"No, I stayed all evening. There was a lot of catching up to do, and the food was excellent, although I missed the opportunity to enjoy the cheese fountain." Virgil's gaze flicked my way.

There was a tap on the door, and Maverick, Cythera's husband, opened it and poked his head around the side. "I'm sorry to interrupt, but the Yule Log ceremony is starting shortly. I thought you'd want to stop to enjoy it."

"Oh! I've been hearing all about that," Virgil said. "It sounds like a fascinating event. I was hoping to attend."

I glanced at Zandra, and she nodded at me. We were done here. Virgil had the power to destroy Habriel, but we couldn't find a solid motive. And just like Bertoli, if they'd gone their separate ways at the end of the night, he couldn't have done it.

"Thanks, Maverick," I said. "We're finished here. We appreciate you being so honest with us, Virgil."

"I'm always honest," he said. "But I wonder if I may ask a small favor."

"Ask away," Zandra said.

"I know you need to question us all about what happened to Habriel, but we've all been looking forward to the Yule Log ceremony and would dearly love to attend. I promise, on my word as a loyal Angel Force employee, that no one will do anything nefarious. I'll make it my personal mission that all the angels you need to speak to will still be here in the morning."

"I can help with that too," Maverick said, still lingering by the door. "And I'll make sure Cythera keeps an eye on things."

We had made plans to meet Tempest and Wiggles at the Yule Log ceremony at midday and then spend time together, and I'd promised Zandra this investigation wouldn't get in the way of festive fun.

"We can pick this up tomorrow. Just make sure everyone is back here bright and early. On your head, be it."

"You have my solemn oath." Virgil pressed a hand against his chest, and snowflakes sparkled around him.

He left with his excitable group of friends, and we updated Cythera as to our progress, or lack thereof. She grunted and complained, but then told us to get lost and stop bothering her.

Maverick kindly escorted us to the exit, mumbling apologies for his wife's rudeness. "My most beloved finds Christmas stressful. And with this unfortunate murder on her hands, she has been snappy."

"We're used to it," I said. "Are you coming to the Yule Log burning?"

"If I can pry my dear sweet Cythera away from her desk, we'll be right behind you."

We said goodbye and headed into the dull, overcast day. It was the perfect conditions to burn the log. People were making their way toward the center of town, where the log would be ceremonially lit. The tradition of burning a Yule log had its roots in winter solstice celebrations and symbolised the return of the sun after the shortest day of the year. We also used this time to ward off evil spirits, the flames demonstrating power and prosperity. And as the ceremony evolved over time, Zandra now got to enjoy slices of chocolate, gooey Yule log cake. It was an evolution she heartily agreed with.

The atmosphere was light-hearted and friendly, despite the recent tragedy. It was a reminder that, even when death visited our town, everyone else's life kept going.

"What did you make of Virgil?" Zandra asked me.

"He came across as honest. And he didn't have to reveal his celestial powers."

"He's either honest or an idiot," she said. "But he has the same alibi as Bertoli."

"It's possible they all went back to the Sleepy Stardust Sanctuary as a group, but then one of them snuck away," I said. "Perhaps whoever killed Habriel knew he planned on stealing the books. They disapproved, so returned to stop him, but there was a struggle."

Zandra quirked an eyebrow. "Do you think it was Virgil?"

"He's super calm if he killed Habriel. I imagine it would take a lot to rile him, especially enough to unleash something as powerful as celestial magic on an old friend."

"They weren't that close, though," Zandra said. "They lost touch after graduation. Maybe Virgil never liked Habriel, and when they reunited at the alumni party, it brought back bad memories."

"If he's concealing his hatred of Habriel, he's doing an excellent job," I said. "And he wasn't at all interested in Habriel's fame."

"He could be secretly jealous," Zandra said. "Virgil has a lackluster career in Angel Force, while Habriel got the fame and glory."

I nodded. "For now, Virgil stays on the suspect list."

As we arrived at the crowded spot where the log would be burned, I spotted Tempest and Wiggles standing off to one side. We headed over to join them. Wiggles rolled around in the snow, while Tempest tossed him treats from a brown paper bag. Her other hand was wrapped around her squirming middle.

"You're still carrying the kittens, I see," I said by way of greeting.

"They're like my own personal hot water bottles," Tempest said with a grin. "How's the investigation going?"

"Let me grab food, and I'll fill you in." While Zandra headed off to get snacks before the log burning, my gaze wandered to the group of angels who'd joined the celebrations. They all appeared excited to be at the event, none of them looking saddened by Habriel's murder.

Something was going on in that friendship group. We hadn't found the right person to question yet, but I'd be keeping an eye on them. One of those angelic creatures had messed up big time, and I was determined to find out which one was the killer.

# Chapter 8

## Morally gray

"Don't get syrup on any of the gifts or the wrapping paper!" Vorana bustled around her kitchen, adding finishing touches to our breakfast before serving. She was multitasking this morning, with one end of the kitchen table dedicated to wrapping Christmas gifts. From the shape of them, it was clear they were books. No surprise there. Vorana loved to pick you the perfect read.

"Don't even think about it," Tempest warned as she scooped a sparking kitten off the table just before it pounced on Wiggles' head. Wiggles had claimed the seat next to Tempest and kept growling at the kittens every time they got too close.

"We're having snowman-shaped pancakes with a side order of clementines to get the vitamins in." Vorana shoved food in front of everyone and then returned to her gift-wrapping task. Naturally, she served Sage and me smoked salmon. Wiggles had pancakes. That hellhound could eat whatever he liked and not have digestive distress.

"It sounds as if this case has got you stumped." Vorana twirled a ribbon around a book-shaped gift.

"We're still early into questioning the suspects," I said, "but so far, they're all telling the same story."

"And if they all have the same story, it means it wasn't an angel Habriel went to the Academy with who committed murder," Zandra said.

Wiggles puffed smoke at a kitten as he tried to steal a piece of pancake off his plate. "Find your own mischief mittens."

"They're not hungry. I already fed them," Tempest said. "They're just curious about what you've got. They think everything is a toy."

"Are you sure you won't take them back with you?" I asked. "You're practically their mother, since you're feeding them as well as carrying them around."

Wiggles stamped a paw, making the table shake. "There's no room for fire-breathing, snack stealing kittens in our lives. Tempest has all the fire-breathing animals she needs. And in case anyone's wondering who that is, that's me. Kittens, take note. You're not wanted."

"You'll hurt their feelings," Vorana said. "Although they are a handful. They set fire to Sage's favorite mat by the back door."

"It had the perfect level of prickle," Sage groused. "I have nowhere comfortable to sleep now."

"Apart from Vorana's bed, all the soft armchairs, the couch, Zandra's bed, if you can be bothered to go down to the basement." I reeled off several more comfy sitting positions.

"None of them are the same as my mat. My Christmas is ruined."

Vorana added more smoked salmon to Sage's plate to placate her. "They're just babies. They're learning how the world works."

"They should learn in someone else's house," Sage said. "Somewhere fireproof."

"I agree," Wiggles said. "They're a distraction we could do without. We haven't finished Christmas shopping. Tempest is so tough to buy for."

"There's time for that," Tempest said. "We're on holiday, so we don't need to rush."

"You're not helping Zandra and Juno solve this murder?" Vorana paused to take a sip of coffee before continuing her present wrapping.

"This is my down time," Tempest said. "Demons get feisty toward the end of the year, so we need to recharge and rest before we go back, all magic blazing, and teach them some manners."

"Then toss them into the prison and never let them out." Wiggles grinned.

"We don't need extra help," Zandra said swiftly. "We've got a handle on things. This isn't the first murder we've solved."

"Exactly. You don't need us," Tempest said.

I was happy to see Tempest giving Zandra free rein in this investigation. Tempest wasn't known for taking a step back and could dominate a situation, especially with Wiggles and his fiery bluntness by her side. But she trusted Zandra to get things right, and I could see from the relieved expression on my wonderful witch's face she was grateful for that.

"What's the next step?" Vorana asked. "Are there more angels to question?"

"Later on," I said. "We're stopping by the Sleepy Stardust Sanctuary to see if Lizzie noticed anything strange going on that night."

"Like an angel creeping out to commit frozen murder?" Tempest raised an eyebrow.

"That's right. The angels we've spoken to so far claim they stayed at the party all night, and they all left together. Habriel was still alive at the end of the evening, so someone must have followed him to his rental or, more likely, snuck out of their hotel room and done the dastardly deed."

"Enjoy," Tempest said. "We're looking around the Christmas market and then heading back to your friend's café."

"She's doing glazed parsnips and ribs as a lunchtime special." Wiggles swiped his tongue over his nose. "I can't wait. I'm having two plates."

"You'll have one plate," Tempest said. "You get gassy when you eat parsnips."

"You're right. One plate of honeyed parsnips and two racks of ribs. That should fill me up for a few hours."

Tempest smirked and rolled her eyes, knowing she had little control over what Wiggles stuffed into his mouth.

With full stomachs, leaving Vorana to her presents, and Tempest and Wiggles to enjoy a day of Christmas shopping, we left the house and began our investigation at the Sleepy Stardust Sanctuary. When we entered the adorable boutique hotel, Lizzie Briar stood behind the desk in the reception area. Garlands and sprigs of holly were hung up, and a cute Christmas tree sparkled in the corner. In the background, Christmas tunes played softly. Lizzie had even dyed the tips of her spiky hair a festive red.

"I was expecting you two to stop by," Lizzie said as we approached.

"Season's greetings!" I said. "I'm sure you've heard the rumors about Habriel. We're in charge of investigating what happened to him."

Lizzie nodded. "I heard. And of course, since his friends are staying here, you'll want the inside scoop, I suppose?"

"Is there an inside scoop?" I hopped onto the desk and sniffed a bowl of candied almonds.

Zandra gently nudged me away from the bowl. "Were you around the night Habriel died?"

"I was on the late shift," Lizzie said. "And I was here when all of Habriel's friends returned from their party. They were in high spirits, laughing and joking. One of them, I think he's called Arioch, danced me around the reception area and snuck a kiss under the mistletoe!"

"They all came back together?" I asked.

"Yes, all accounted for. They'd left their keys here so they wouldn't lose them. I handed them all back."

"The angel who died wasn't staying here, though," Zandra said.

"That's right. Although he'd made inquiries about renting a place, so I told him what was available. We don't have many suitable rentals that big, but Habriel got what he wanted. I was surprised he booked something so large, since he was the only one staying there."

"Do you have the address?" I asked.

"I already wrote it down in case you came asking." Lizzie handed over a piece of paper. The address was in the posh part of Crimson Cove. I didn't recognize the name of the house, but when houses came with names, you knew they weren't going to be small or cheap.

"Did you stay up all night?" Zandra asked.

"I did. I worked from ten pm until four am." Lizzie pulled a face. "There's never much happening around that time. Most of the guests have turned in for the night. It was quiet, nothing exciting going on. I'm usually super tired the next day, though, but I felt refreshed. Maybe it was the angel's kiss that gave me a boost. They're all so handsome, aren't they?"

"I've never met a gross one," I said. "Did any of them leave the hotel?"

"No. Once they got to their bedrooms, everything went silent. They're the only guests staying and have taken all the rooms. They grabbed their keys and headed off to bed."

"There must be a back way out of here," I said. "Could someone have snuck down the stairs and got out that way?"

Lizzie shook her head. "That door is locked. Guests know not to use it after a certain hour or they'll set off an alarm. It's front door only at night."

"Did you fall asleep at the desk?" I asked.

"No! I admit to occasionally nodding off when it gets silent, but not that night. Maybe I'm full of

Christmas cheer, but I felt really good that evening, and the next day. I promise I didn't fall asleep."

"We're missing an obvious point," Zandra said. "Angels have wings. They could have flown out of an upstairs window."

Lizzie squinted and pursed her lips. "The guests can open and close their windows, but it would be a squeeze for an angel to get out of one. This is an old building, and I had to keep the original features during the redesign. That includes the tiny windows."

"We need to test that theory," I said. "Lizzie, may we borrow your snow globe?"

"Help yourself." She pushed it my way.

I made a call to Angel Force and was put through to Bertoli. "We need your urgent assistance at the Sleepy Stardust Sanctuary."

"Have you found a clue?"

"Possibly. But we need an angel to see if our theory is correct."

"I'll be right there." And true to his word, Bertoli landed less than two minutes later outside the sanctuary, kicking up snow with his impressive landing skills. He strode inside and walked over to us. "What's going on? What did you find? It wasn't one of my friends, was it?"

Zandra looked amused as she took a step back. "I'm leaving this to you, Juno. It was your crazy idea."

"We have a theory to test. Come upstairs." I trotted up the stairs, with Bertoli in the middle and Zandra taking up the rear. There was a window at the end of the corridor, and sure enough, as Lizzie described, it was surprisingly small. I pointed a paw at the window. "Get through that."

Bertoli looked startled. "If I squeeze through that window, I could damage my wings."

"Give it a try. You're flexible."

He walked to the window and opened it. "I'm telling you, I won't fit. Why don't you do it?"

"We're wondering if one of your friends used a window to creep out of and go after Habriel," Zandra said.

Recognition dawned in Bertoli's eyes, but he immediately shook his head. "It wasn't any of my friends. None of us wanted to hurt Habriel. We were all stunned by what happened."

"Stunned but not sad," I said. "I studied everyone's expressions when Habriel was discovered frozen in the middle of town. Yes, there was shock and disbelief, but none of you shed a tear. Isn't that strange, given how close you were all supposed to be?"

Bertoli blinked several times. "We are sad. I am, anyway. And like you said, we were in shock. People react differently when shock hits."

"Yet you all acted the same," I said. "Nobody cried. That's odd. Now, help us test the theory that an angel murdered Habriel."

Bertoli looked puzzled, his forehead furrowed, and his mouth turned down. He opened his mouth then snapped it shut.

"Is there something you'd like to share with us?" I asked. "Do you know what happened to Habriel?"

"No! I'm telling you, this won't work, but I'll do it so you know no angel staying here had anything to do with Habriel's murder."

I exchanged a pointed look with Zandra. That statement put Bertoli at the top of the suspect list. All of Habriel's friends, apart from Bertoli, were staying at the Sleepy Stardust Sanctuary, which meant he had no alibi. He'd gone home alone to his apartment. He could have easily snuck out and tackled Habriel without anybody seeing.

But Bertoli appeared unaware he'd made himself suspect number one as he hoisted onto the window ledge and forced himself through. He got both shoulders out, but then his wings got wedged.

"Keep squirming," I said. "Tuck your wings in tighter. You can make it."

"I'm stuck! This is ridiculous. Even if one of my friends got out of this window, there's no room to spread my wings. I'd fall. And it's not high enough to leap from."

"Come back inside. We've seen enough," Zandra said.

"Let him wriggle for a few more seconds," I said. "Bertoli has the peachiest butt."

"Hey! Stop looking at my butt!"

I chuckled.

Bertoli flailed about. "You'll have to pull me. I really am stuck."

Zandra grabbed Bertoli's legs and yanked him hard. He shot backward out of the window and landed on top of her, so his wings were squashing her face.

"You should release my wonderful witch with the greatest of speed, unless you want to get zapped in that peachy behind with a particularly painful spell," I said.

Bertoli rolled off of Zandra and held out his hand, mumbling an apology. "I knew that wouldn't work."

She caught hold of his hand and pulled herself up. "If all the windows are this size, sneaking out wouldn't work."

"Let's check the back door to see if it was tampered with, but if none of the angels staying here left, that leaves us with a tricky situation." I stared hard at Bertoli, but he wasn't getting the point.

After we'd inspected the back door and determined it was untouched, Bertoli headed back to Angel Force. After saying goodbye to Lizzie, we took a brisk twenty-minute walk to the house Habriel rented.

"It can't be Bertoli," Zandra said.

"I agree, but we shouldn't ignore the clues, or we'll be no better than Cythera."

She puffed out a breath. "He wouldn't. He's a stickler for the rules."

"Then he needs to give us a decent alibi." I picked up the pace. "Hurry! We can worry about how guilty Bertoli is after snooping through Habriel's belongings."

The doors and windows of the rental were locked, but with a simple spell, it was easy to gain access.

"This angel had serious money to burn." Zandra turned slowly in the plush living room with its exquisite baby pink velvet couches and original oil paintings mounted on the wall.

The house had the air of a temporary home rather than one loved by anyone. All the rooms were tastefully decorated, but it was all neutral. There were no personal effects dotted around.

We investigated the downstairs and found nothing useful then headed upstairs and explored the six bedrooms and three bathrooms.

"This must have been the room Habriel used." There were a few items of clothing tossed around and a small bag with overnight supplies in it. I checked in the bathroom. There were several small gray feathers on the tiled floor. I sniffed them. They had a hint of angel about them, but there was something less pleasant mingled in with the scent.

"Angels don't go gray, do they?" I asked Zandra as she appeared in the bathroom doorway.

"Honestly, I don't know. They're mainly blond, so it's hard to see any gray hair. The higher angels aren't gray, and they're ancient."

"These feathers must belong to someone else," I said.

Zandra looked in the bathroom cabinet. She lifted out a bottle. "Maybe they do go gray. This is dye. Was Habriel going prematurely gray?"

"He looked like a natural blond to me," I said. "Perhaps it was left behind by a previous tenant?"

We searched some more but found no useful clues. Zandra took one of the feathers, though, just in case it led us to something useful.

"So, no one snuck out of the Sleepy Stardust Sanctuary," Zandra said, "and there's no sign of a fight here. Yet Habriel found himself back in town after the party ended, holding a stolen book, and getting himself frozen to death."

I twitched my whiskers. "Let's continue talking to the suspects. One of them must slip up soon, and when they do, we'll pounce."

# Chapter 9

## Portal problem

"Arioch was supposed to be here ten minutes ago." Zandra paced the interview room, stopping by the door and yanking it open. "I thought angels were good timekeepers. Keeping us waiting is rude. I want to be drinking hot chocolate with whipped cream and cinnamon sugar sprinkles, not stuck interrogating potentially murderous angels."

I sat on the interview table, my tail neatly wrapped around my front paws. "If he doesn't show up soon, it'll make me suspicious of why he's avoiding us. Could he be the guilty angel we're looking for?"

We'd set out a timetable of interviews for the rest of the angels from Bertoli's alumni party, so we could get through them quickly and see which one wasn't telling the truth. We planned on interviewing Arioch, followed by Nisroc, then Tabris, and finally Sorush. That would keep us busy for the rest of the day, especially when we had to unpick their stories to find the hole that would lead us to the killer.

"I saw a plate of Christmas sugar cookies in the kitchen," I said. "You should ask Bertoli to bring them in for you to enjoy."

"I've had enough sugar."

"I didn't think that was possible," I teased.

She smirked at me. "At last! Here he is."

Arioch strode into the open-plan office. He was similar in appearance to the other angels. Above-average height, sparkling white wings, and a gleaming smile. What I hadn't noticed before, though, was the coldness in his blue eyes. Most angels were friendly, and since many went into careers in law enforcement, it paid to have a welcoming demeanor. Not this one. Arioch strutted through the office, greeting no one, and headed straight for the interview room.

"What kept you?" Zandra asked as she settled in her seat.

Arioch flipped around his chair and straddled it. "I almost didn't bother coming. This is a waste of my time. And I'm busy."

"Is there somewhere important you need to be?" I narrowed my eyes, not liking his off-hand manner.

"Anywhere but here. I didn't even want to go to the party, but Habriel twisted my arm. Look where it landed me."

"You're not a social butterfly?" I asked.

He snorted in response. "You have questions for me?"

"Let's start at the beginning," I said. "How did you know Habriel?"

"The same as the others. We met at the Academy."

"You said he twisted your arm to come here. That must mean you were in regular contact, even though he decided not to stay in Angel Force."

"Sure. But I wouldn't say we were best buddies, more like friendly rivals," Arioch said.

"Explain that relationship further," Zandra said. "Rivalry suggests tension."

"You can call it that if you like." Arioch shrugged. "We all need someone in our lives to push us to be a better person. That's what Habriel did for me. We did it for each other."

"In all areas of your life?" I asked.

"I'm not interested in music, if that's what you mean," Arioch said. "But we'd catch up every couple of months. Habriel would tell me about the amazing things he'd done, and I'd share my own stories."

"It was a case of one-upmanship? Habriel had this glittering rockstar career, and you were jealous?"

"Jealous of what? He was welcome to his glittering rockstar career, as you put it," Arioch said. "He was in the limelight and on public display, and I'd find that tedious. Habriel was always doing some kind of promotion or going on photo shoots because he was endorsing some product or other. That wasn't a life I aspired to."

"Since Habriel had to convince you to come to the party, you don't enjoy those, either?" I asked.

"I like the guys at the party well enough, but spending a whole night with them, with no way to escape and recharge, did my head in. I prefer my own company. It's the best company you'll find around here."

Arioch sounded like an introvert, but an arrogant one. He was happy to minimize social contact with others and content to spend his time alone recharging his batteries. Zandra could be like that sometimes, so I understood his standpoint.

"Where would you and Habriel meet when you had your catch ups?" Zandra asked.

"It varied, depending on where he was and my work schedule," Arioch said. "I don't know why you're interested in that. How is it relevant to what happened to the guy?"

"We're getting a full picture of Habriel's life," Zandra said. "We need to find out if anyone had issues with him."

"Someone obviously did, since he got himself frozen to death after stealing those dumb books," Arioch replied.

"Did Habriel tell you he planned to take the books?" I asked.

"No, but it would be the sort of sneaky thing he'd do. Not out of malice, but because he knew it would cause a stir. He found Angel Force and the Academy ways restraining. He used to make fun of them with me in secret."

"You don't like Angel Force either?" Zandra asked.

"They gave me this career, so I've no complaints," Arioch said. "But anyone who's been working for them for a while will complain about the layers of bureaucracy and the dumb forms we need to fill out if we want so much as a new uniform. Some of the departments still don't use electronics because the magic fries them without the right tech guards in place. It's frustratingly old-fashioned. I'm always talking about how we need to update and improve, but no one listens to me."

"Did Habriel listen?" I asked. "Was he someone you turned to when you had a complaint?"

"It wasn't that kind of friendship. We'd egg each other on, not pat each other on the back. I once went for a promotion because Habriel said I'd never get it. I wanted to prove him wrong."

"And did you get it?" I asked.

"I got the job," Arioch said with a smug smile. "And I was happy to rub his nose in it. The arrogant son of a gun told me that's exactly what he had planned all along. He knew if he goaded me enough, I'd do it. But it was the same with his first single. He kept messing around with the song, tinkering and saying it wasn't good enough. In the end, I told him he'd definitely fail if he didn't get it out there. But he whined and moaned for another few weeks until I turned on him and told him he was a talentless grunt and the song was the worst thing I'd ever heard. Do you know what happened next?"

"Habriel released his hit single. And the rest is history?"

"You got it in one. Now, are we done? I've got somewhere I need to be." Arioch rose from the chair, but Zandra gestured for him to sit back down.

"We have a few more questions. Did you see Habriel leave the party at any point?"

"We didn't hang out all night, but as far as I know, we all stayed there," Arioch said. "It was freezing outside and snowing for most of the night, so none of us wanted to go out for a late-night fly."

"Does that mean you stayed inside at the party all night as well?" I asked.

He nodded, his gaze narrowing. "Don't try to pin this on me. I may not have the best performance record, but I wouldn't kill an old friend."

"What's wrong with your performance record?" I jumped on the admission he wasn't a perfect angel.

"I figured you'd have dug into that by now," Arioch said with a sigh. "You know how Angel Force loves to keep records."

"We're looking into everyone who had a close connection to Habriel," Zandra said. "But why don't you tell us to save time?"

He shrugged again. "I sometimes don't follow the rules. And Angel Force has a lot of rules. My instructors at the Academy always told me I had a big mouth, and little has changed."

"You've had warnings for bad behavior?" I asked.

"This and that," Arioch admitted, "but nothing to get me kicked out of Angel Force. And I secured that promotion, so they must think I'm decent at my job."

A troubled angel with a questionable attitude. Perhaps Arioch's rivalry with Habriel hadn't had such a friendly edge. They could have been bitter rivals and things came to a head at the party. But how did Arioch sneak out of the Sleepy Stardust Sanctuary to kill Habriel?

"Do you know anyone who had a problem with Habriel?" Zandra asked. "A problem big enough to want him dead?"

Arioch's nose twitched from side to side. "When a guy gets that famous, he's bound to annoy some people. Have you spoken to the others at the party?"

"We're working our way through his closest friends," I said.

Arioch hesitated. "Does anyone stand out?"

"Should anyone?"

"That's not for me to say." He glanced around the room. "We were all friends. And we were all at the party. Don't single me out because I've made a few bad career moves."

I got the impression Arioch was hiding something from us, but he didn't trust us enough to share.

He pushed away from the chair. "Now, I really do need to go. I can't miss my time slot."

"For what?" Zandra asked.

Arioch's expression went blank. "It's personal. And it's got nothing to do with what happened to Habriel." Without waiting for permission, he strode out of the interview room.

"There's something seriously off with that guy." Zandra's gaze was fixed on Arioch's back. "I felt an alert ping inside me the second he arrived, but I can't figure out the problem. Why would an angel make me wary?"

"I got the same impression," I said. "I don't trust Arioch. We should find out what this personal business is."

"You want to tail him?"

I hopped off the table. "We need to. And we're not interviewing Nisroc for another hour, so we have time."

We told Cythera what we were doing, and she grumpily waved us away. It was a bright, sunny day, but still bitingly cold, and I was happy to hop onto Zandra's shoulder to keep both of us warm. We kept a healthy distance from Arioch as he strutted ahead of us.

"This guy is definitely going somewhere in a hurry," Zandra said. "Maybe he knows someone in town."

"I've never seen him visit Crimson Cove, but it's possible he has a connection to the local branch of Angel Force," I said.

"So why not meet his friend at the office, since he was going to be there, anyway?" Zandra asked. "This is shady behavior."

Arioch stopped and pulled a small piece of paper out of his pocket. He studied it for a few seconds, walked to the next alleyway that divided two stores, and slipped into it. We were hot on his heels, stopping by the entrance to the alleyway to see who he was meeting.

There was no one there. Arioch stood alone, staring at a brick wall.

"What's this guy playing at?" Zandra whispered.

We ducked out of sight as Arioch glanced along the alley. I counted to five before peeking back around the corner. Arioch had his hands raised over his head, his palms facing upward. His head was tipped back, and I could see he was speaking.

"He's casting a spell!" Zandra said. "I can't hear the words, though."

"But I feel the magic," I said. "That's not angel magic he's using. Do you sense it?"

Zandra lifted a hand and inhaled deeply. "It's gray magic! An angel with the ability to channel gray magic?"

Gray spells came at a price. They weren't as dark as the powerfully twisted spells used by some, but whenever you cast a gray magic spell, you or someone close to you paid the price. It could be as simple as an illness or a small misfortune, but no one used gray magic lightly because of the consequences.

Arioch flared his wings and brought his hands down, a cascade of swirling gray sparkles shooting out toward the wall. The magic built in intensity until it formed a circle.

"He's opening a portal!" I tensed, my fur standing on end. "We have a rogue angel on our hands. Angels aren't permitted to open portals without authorization."

"And from what he told us in his interview, he's not the type to get authorization for something like this," Zandra said.

"I can only imagine the paperwork involved." Angels only used portals in extreme circumstances because it was such taxing magic. It wasn't like casting a translocation spell that moved you from one place to another. Angels opened portals if they wanted to go to a realm outside of their control. A realm they were often not welcome in.

"We have to stop Arioch from going through," I said. "If he's not in control of this portal, anything could creep out. The town is at risk."

Zandra nodded. "Let's get him and shake the truth out of him."

I flared my magic at the same time as Zandra, testing our bond to ensure it was sure and steady. Zandra blasted out a knock back spell, which caught Arioch's attention, though he barely moved, despite the power of Zandra's magic hitting him.

He scowled at us when he realized he wasn't alone. "Get out of here. It's not safe."

"And it's not safe for you to open a portal in our town." I leaped off Zandra's shoulder with my murder mittens outstretched and latched onto Arioch's flared wing. He hissed in pain just as Zandra unleashed a volley of knock back spells, sending him reeling. Arioch pitched over and hit the ground, huffing out a pained grunt.

I briefly removed my teeth from his wing. "Care to explain what you're doing and where you were about to go?"

# Chapter 10

## Angel down

"Let go of me! I must get through the portal." Arioch struggled to break free, but with Zandra pinning him down with not only magic but also her boot, he was going nowhere.

"You're using gray magic." My murder mittens were still firmly attached to his wing.

"I wasn't! This is a mistake." Arioch writhed but was unable to break free.

"The huge swirling portal that leads you to who knows where tells another story," Zandra said. "What are you playing at messing with that sort of magic in our town?"

"I... I messed up. It's easily done. A friend gave me the spell to try. It must have been a joke."

"No one gives a gray magic spell that opens a portal as a joke," I said. "Who is this friend?"

"I forget. It's not important. Just let me go, and I'll explain everything."

"You'll jump through the portal, and we'll never see you again," Zandra said. "Until you tell us the truth, you're staying in the dirt and getting a closeup of my boot."

Arioch's anxious gaze went to the portal. "This is important."

"So you know what it's for and where it goes," I said. "You're a shady angel. Did Habriel find out you were dabbling in gray magic?"

"Habriel! This has nothing to do with him," Arioch said.

"Perhaps he saw you using powers you shouldn't and decided to get rid of his friendly rival," Zandra said. "We only have your word for it that you were actually friends. He caught you out just like we've done and planned on bringing you in. If Angel Force learns about this, you'll be out of a job."

"Habriel never knew I used this kind of magic," Arioch said. "And even if he did, it wouldn't give me a reason to kill him. He pulled dubious stunts all the time."

"Like what?" I asked.

Arioch grunted. "With his groupies. I only know about it because he bragged to me. But if that news hit the headlines, his career would have been over. I could have ruined him without taking his life, but I didn't do it."

"It's over now because somebody close to Habriel murdered him," I said.

"And we think that someone could be you," Zandra said.

"Maybe it was somebody he knew, but not me," Arioch said. "Let me go. I have to get through before it's too late."

"Not until you tell us everything about the night Habriel was killed," Zandra said.

"I already have! I was at the party with everybody else. Most of us arrived together, we all stayed till the end, and then we went back to the hotel as a group. That's it. I don't know what happened to Habriel on his way home, but it had nothing to do with me."

"What did you do when you got back to the hotel?" I asked.

"The same as everybody. It had been a long day, and all I wanted to do was crash."

"Are you sure you didn't cast any portal-creating gray magic?"

He huffed out a breath. "You can believe what you like, but just let me up. I'm innocent, and you're invading my personal space."

Neither of us backed down. If Arioch was content to risk getting his wings singed by gray power, it wasn't that big of a stretch to imagine him taking another angel's life if they got in the way of his plans. And whatever those plans were, they lay on the other side of the portal.

Arioch sensed this wasn't going his way and relaxed. But then he sprang up, taking us both by surprise. The air crackled with energy as he launched himself at us, his wings unfurling in a display of power. I had to act fast to stop him from getting the upper hand, so I drew upon my ancient magic, my fur standing on end as I prepared to unleash a barrage of spells.

Zandra raised her hands and a swirling vortex of energy erupted between us, slamming into Arioch with a deafening force. He let out a cry of pain, his wings faltering as he was pushed back.

Without missing a beat, I leaped forward, my claws glowing with a bright blue light. I slashed at Arioch's chest, my magic lashing out like razor-sharp talons. He hissed in agony, retaliating with a blast of energy that sent me flying backward.

I landed on my paws, my heart pounding. Zandra was already weaving another spell, her brow furrowed in concentration. I launched myself at Arioch again, dodging his attacks as I searched for an opening. Zandra's spells rained down around us, creating a dizzying display of light and shadow.

Our magic clashed and sparked. Arioch's attack grew more frantic as Zandra and I pushed him back, farther from the portal. He lashed out with bursts of light, but I kept one step ahead of his strikes. Zandra's spell wrapped around Arioch, binding his wings and sapping his strength.

He let out a guttural roar, and with a final, desperate surge of power, he broke free from Zandra's bindings and charged toward the portal. We couldn't let him escape, so I gathered my magical energy and unleashed it in a devastating blast.

The air crackled and thundered as my spell collided with Arioch's power and slowed him. Zandra dodged in front of the portal, blocking his escape. He lunged at her, sending them both through the portal.

My heart skittered as I leapt after my witch. Where she went, so did I. The world tilted. A rainbow of colors flashed in front of me, and my stomach flipped several times. This portal journey was rough and unpleasant.

I landed on a pile of white angel wings. For a second, I thought it was Arioch and prepared to strike, but this angel reeked of illness and weakness.

I sprang off and landed on crunchy gravel that was hot beneath my paws. The angel I'd landed on peered up at me from her crouched position, her pale skin grubby and her blue eyes dull. She cowered away. Since she appeared to be no threat, I raced over to where Zandra and Arioch were battling.

Zandra wove intricate patterns in the air, her fingers trailing wisps of purple smoke. Arioch's wings unfurled, each feather glowing. The air crackled and hissed, raw energy lashing out in unpredictable arcs. Zandra ducked as a bolt of celestial ice shot at her. Arioch grunted, and their eyes locked, both searching for any sign of weakness.

My muscles coiled, ready to spring. One more heartbeat, and I would join the fray and we'd obliterate Arioch.

Zandra threw out a fierce spell that knocked Arioch down, and I landed on him, spiralling out a carpet of draining magic. I raised a murder mitten, ready to strike.

"Please, don't harm him," the female angel I'd landed on called out as she crawled closer. "He's protecting me."

Arioch's head whipped around at the sound of the other angel's voice, and he looked torn between wanting to continue the battle and helping her.

Eventually, he sighed, and the fight drained out of him. "Enough! She's the reason I had to get through the portal. I can only access the portal into this realm twice a day. I was so worried about her the last time we met that I couldn't risk missing my slot."

Zandra flipped her hair out of her face. "Where are we?"

"A bad place," the female angel whispered. "Arioch, you shouldn't have come. I told you to stay away."

"I need to check on Dina." Arioch held up his hands in a gesture of defeat. "I won't try anything funny, and you can see she needs help. She's got no one else looking out for her."

Zandra nodded at me, and I bounced off Arioch. He rolled to his feet and hurried to Dina, talking softly as he crouched in front of her.

"Wherever we've landed, it's giving me major heebie-jeebies," Zandra said to me. "I get the sense we're being watched, and whatever's watching us isn't friendly."

Now I had a moment to breathe, I surveyed the landscape. This realm was dark, with no signs of nature blossoming. All the trees looked dead and sickly. The ground was covered in strange, crunchy gravel that was hot and unpleasantly sharp against my toe beans.

"We don't want to stay here any longer than we have to," I said.

"We can't leave," Arioch said. "Dina's not stable enough to travel through a portal. She needs more healing magic."

"I need to stay. My work isn't finished." Dina's voice was a hoarse croak.

"No, we've talked about this. You agreed you would come back with me." Arioch forced Dina to look at him. "Remember?"

"You work in this dreary realm?" I asked. "What do you do here?"

"Give me a few minutes to give Dina an energy boost, then I'll explain it all." Arioch cast several spells over the angel. Her complexion brightened a fraction, but she still seemed dangerously weak. He finally turned to us, resting a hand on one of Dina's shoulders.

I curled my tail around my paws and waited for answers.

Arioch's mouth puckered. "The portal we came through brought us into a demon realm."

"Oh! That makes sense. It's why I'm getting the heebie-jeebies." Zandra grimaced.

"You work with demons?" I asked Dina.

She nodded but gestured for Arioch to continue, as if saying more than a few words was too much effort.

"Dina used to teach at the Academy," he said. "I met her when I was a student. She was my primary tutor for my final dissertation. We got along. We have the same sense of humor and a mind for rebelling against the more pointless rules Angel Force put into place."

"And your academic work brought you here?" I asked Dina. "Your profession is doing you no favors."

"I'm an anthropologist," she said. "I study archaic civilizations before they die out. This particular realm is ruled by Harzies demons. Have you heard of them?"

My heart clenched as an icy finger of fear wrapped around it. "Harzie demons. That translates into heart seize. They were exterminated. They had to be."

"Tempest told me about those demons." Zandra looked up, appearing to dredge her memories. "Something about them destroying dreams and sowing despair. Is that right?"

Dina nodded. "They are small, with no obvious killing tools, such as claws or fangs, but they have the power to see into a person's thoughts, take their dreams, and twist them into tragedies. For a long time, they were free to roam because people thought they were no threat. That was until they took over the hearts of a minor royal family and attempted to start a war with their neighbors."

"That's right," I said. "They almost destroyed two nations. That was when the order came to remove them all."

"And that order was carried out," Arioch said. "It should have been a success."

"Hardy civilizations find a way to survive," Dina said. "And I have a fascination with archaic civilizations that refuse to adapt to ensure they thrive."

"A handful of Harzies demons fled the extermination order," Arioch said. "They created this realm for themselves. Dina discovered it and requested an invitation to live among them."

"Why would you want to do that?" Zandra asked.

"It's common with anthropologists," I said. "Living among the community they wish to study and assimilating into it is the most effective means of research."

Dina nodded again. "To begin with, it worked. The demons were puzzled by my interest and naturally wary, thinking I was here to carry out an extermination order from Angel Force, but they began to trust me, and I them."

"That's when it all went wrong," Arioch said. "When Dina's time came to leave, they refused to let her go. They've been punishing her ever since by sucking out her hope and replacing it with a crippling despair."

"Tempest and Wiggles need to know about this place," Zandra said. "These demons can't be allowed to get away with imprisoning angels."

"Tempest? Wiggles? Do you mean Tempest Crypt and her hound?" A flicker of recognition entered Dina's eyes before she cowered and hissed. "Crypt witches. There's a Crypt witch close by?"

"You're looking at one. Well, one who was raised by them," I said. "Zandra Crypt is the most wonderful and all-powerful witch you'll ever have the privilege of meeting."

Dina turned panicked eyes to Arioch. "She'll destroy my work. We can't let it happen. The Crypt witches despise demons."

"They won't ruin all of your hard work," Arioch said.

"We might. After all, we didn't want to come here. You shoved my witch through the gray portal," I said.

Arioch scowled at me. "Even if they do, if you're destroyed by insisting on staying here, nothing will be gained. Please, tell me you're ready to leave." Arioch was on his knees, almost begging.

"I needed my journals."

"Did you get them?" Arioch asked.

"One was destroyed in a fire, but the rest are here." Dina patted the satchel slung over her shoulder.

"You've been using gray magic to access this portal in an attempt to get Dina free?" I asked Arioch.

He was already helping Dina to put an arm around his shoulder, so she could stand. "Of course. I don't use magic like that for fun. I told you I broke a few rules, and I'm breaking this one to save someone important to me. Dina saw my potential when nobody else did. She let me study the way I needed to, to ensure I graduated with honors."

"You were an excellent student," Dina said. "And you've turned into an even more exceptional man."

"You'll have time to sing each other's praises on the other side of the portal." Zandra was looking around. "Something is coming."

I was also on the alert, as the sounds of things creeping toward us grew louder, the soft scrape of something sharp sliding across the hot stone.

"Then we must move." Arioch was already pulling Dina to her feet.

"Zandra, you help Arioch. I'll hold the demons off." I powered up and flared magic around me.

The light revealed six pairs of eyes fixed on us. "Go! Get back to the portal."

"You come, too!" Zandra yelled.

Before I had a chance to respond, the first demon pounced. My claws extended, crackling with energy as I met the demon in mid-air. Its fetid breath washed over me as we tumbled, my magic searing its leathery hide. I twisted, breaking free, only to face another attacker.

Two more demons lunged from the shadows. I arched my back and released a burst of energy. It caught one square in the chest, flinging it back into the darkness with a shriek. The other demon raked my flank with a pronged piece of metal, drawing out a hiss of pain.

My tail lashed as I spun, teeth bared. Magic pulsed through me, each heartbeat sending waves of power to my murder mittens. I leaped, bouncing between two demons, my claws leaving glowing trails in the air. They howled, the acrid smell of singed demon flesh filling my booping snooter.

A larger demon, eyes gleaming with malevolence, charged. This wasn't a harzie demon. I barely had time to brace myself before its massive form slammed into me. We rolled, a tangle of fur, claws, and gnashing teeth. Its hot breath was on my neck, jaws snapping inches from my throat. With a yowl of defiance, I channeled my magic into an explosive burst, propelling the beast off me.

Panting, I scrambled to my paws. The remaining demons circled, wary now of the small cat that packed such a powerful punch. My sides heaved, my flesh stinging where the demon's weapon had made its mark.

As two demons rushed me from opposite sides, I waited until the last second before leaping. They collided beneath me with a sickening crunch. I landed on the back of one, my magically charged claws sinking deep into its flesh.

But the demons' numbers seemed endless, their relentless assault pushing me back step by step. There were more than a few harzie demons living here. And it seemed they'd been making friends and offering places to stay to other demons.

My magic flickered, and I knew I couldn't hold out much longer. But Zandra was safe. She'd made it through the portal, and that was where I needed to be.

"Juno!" Zandra's desperate cry pierced through the chaos. "Get to the portal! It's about to close."

I chanced a glance over my shoulder, spotting the shimmering entrance shrinking. I unleashed a blinding flash of light, momentarily stunning my attackers, then bolted, my paws barely touching the crunchy ground as I raced toward salvation.

But the demons recovered quickly. They swarmed after me, their howls of rage filling the air. My legs burned, and my lungs heaved as I pushed myself to my limit. The portal was so close, yet with each stride, it seemed to grow more distant.

A demon's claw snagged my tail, yanking me back. I yowled in pain and frustration, twisting to face my pursuers. They surrounded me, their eyes gleaming with triumph as they closed in. The portal pulsed tantalizingly close, but it was just out of my reach.

A brilliant purple light cut through the darkness, and a rope of magical energy snaked past me, wrapping around my midsection. I felt a powerful tug, and then I was airborne, sailing over the heads of the astonished demons.

"I've got you!" Zandra shouted, her face contorted with effort as she reeled me in.

I flew through the air, the demons' howls of fury fading behind me, and shot through the portal as it disintegrated, tumbling into Zandra's waiting arms. We fell backward, the portal sealing shut behind me with a thunderous boom. For a moment, we lay there, panting and trembling. Then, as the realization of our narrow escape sank in, I nuzzled into Zandra's embrace. We'd made it. We were safe.

Dina lay on her back, staring at the sky. "I've never seen anything more beautiful in my life. I thought I would die in that place."

"You nearly did," Arioch said.

"You're not the only one." Zandra still had me wrapped in her arms, but she reached out and shoved Arioch. "Juno almost died because you've been keeping secrets. You're reckless and stupid."

He turned to us, a flicker of regret in his eyes. "I promise I'm not keeping any secrets about Habriel. I didn't murder him because he learned about my use of gray magic. He liked Dina, too."

"Habriel? Your friend from the Academy? He's dead?" Dina looked horrified at the news.

"There's a lot I need to fill you in on," Arioch said. "First, let's get you somewhere warm. You need a bath, some food, and then bed."

Dina didn't protest, whispering her thanks to us as Arioch guided her along the alley. He turned back. "Have you spoken to Nisroc?"

"Not yet." I was inspecting my flank wound. "He's next on our list."

"I'm... I'm not saying he had anything to do with Habriel's murder, but they argued at the party. I don't know what it was about, and he's not the kind of guy to hold a grudge, but maybe something else happened between them. I don't know. You'll have to ask him."

"I know the angel you speak of," Dina said. "Nisroc was always a good boy, but Habriel wasn't kind to him. Habriel had a bright spark, but it burned too hot, and I had to reprimand him several times because he bullied other students."

"That's enough talking. Let's get you looked after." Arioch nodded goodbye as they left the alley.

I blew out a breath and then scrambled onto Zandra's shoulder. "That was an interesting turn of events."

"A portal, demons, and the angels are turning on each other." Zandra nodded. "This is progress. First things first, we need to tell Tempest and Wiggles about this demon portal. It needs shutting for good."

"And then we're speaking to Nisroc about why he argued with Habriel," I said.

"No, we're healing your injuries."

"I'm fine."

"You're bleeding."

"I'll feel better after a plate of salmon. A large plate."

"Healing. Salmon. A chocolate tiffin for me. And then, we're interrogating Nisroc."

I purred softly. How did I get to have such a truly wonderful witch?

# Chapter 11

# No show

"What is it with these angels and their inability to show up when they're supposed to?" Zandra drained her mug of coffee and thumped it down on the kitchen counter.

We'd been waiting twenty minutes at Angel Force for Nisroc to show up for his interview.

"Is this another one we should be worried about?" I asked. "Especially since Arioch pointed the finger at him."

"With good reason," Zandra said. "Dina revealed Habriel was the Academy's bully. Bullies leave scars. Even if they think they're just messing around and showing off in front of their friends, their version of entertainment is always cruel."

"And their victims have long memories," I said. "The bullies forget, but the damage has been done."

"Just when we think we've got the angels figured out, they surprise us," Zandra said. "They're supposed to be these beings full of light and goodness, but the guys we've spoken to so far all have flaws."

I hopped onto the counter and snooped around for suitable treats. "No one is flawless."

"Not even you?"

I twitched my booping snooter. "Perhaps because I admit to my faults, it means I am flawless."

"Whatever you say," Zandra said with an exaggerated eye roll. "We should go look for Nisroc. Find out what's holding him up."

There was a yelp from the open-plan office, and something crashed to the floor. A few seconds later, Wiggles appeared in the kitchen doorway.

"Greetings! How was the portal?" I asked him.

His nose wrinkled. "Bleurgh! You still stink of demon."

"I'll have a bath later. Did you deal with the portal?"

"Piece of cake. It took us ten minutes to seal it for good, then we went back to the Christmas market. They have these foot long sausages. So good. Anyway, I'm not here to talk sausage. You've got to watch the marshmallow eating contest! I convinced Tempest to enter, and I'm doing it, too."

"Then naturally, you'll win," I said. "You have a bottomless pit for a stomach and a love of all things sweet."

Wiggles wagged his stubby tail. "I'll let the competition have a fair shot, but this prize is in the bag. Hurry! It starts in five minutes, and I don't want to miss my slot." He turned and bounded away through the office, causing more angels to skitter to one side to avoid being trampled. Another full trash can went flying.

"A ten-minute break won't hurt," Zandra said. "And it'll be fun to watch Tempest and Wiggles stuff their faces."

"While we're out, we can keep watch for Nisroc." I hopped onto Zandra's shoulder, and after letting Cythera know we'd be back soon, we headed outside.

The afternoon was crisp and bright. Despite the recent murder, there was an air of cheerfulness as we hurried to catch up with Wiggles. The marshmallow eating contest was taking place in Verity Yummy's English themed tearoom, and a small crowd had gathered, ready to watch eight plucky individuals sitting at tables with huge piles of white and pink marshmallows in front of them.

Wiggles hopped onto the empty seat next to Tempest, who looked like she wanted to be anywhere else but there. He whispered in her ear, and she grimaced but nodded.

Zandra grabbed a hot chocolate, and we eased our way to the front of the crowd to watch the fun.

Verity sidled up to us a few seconds later. She was a pretty, vivacious magic user with red hair. "I'm glad you're here."

"I couldn't miss watching my sister make an idiot of herself." Zandra pointed at Tempest.

"I just wanted to say thank you again for everything you did for me. You know, with the whole weird behavior thing."

"Although it's appreciated, you've already said thank you many times," I said.

Verity smiled. "And I mean every one of them. It was a terrible thing, with Nahla and Petra's murders happening so soon after I opened my tearoom. I thought it would be bad for business, but it's been the opposite. People still talk about what happened during that awful time."

"People are ghoulish," I said. "Although I'm happy for you that a double murder was good for the tearoom."

"I don't promote it!" Verity looked startled. "But if people ask, I tell them what happened. And Ivan was thrilled to have his murder conviction against Petra squashed. That was all thanks to you."

"How's Ivan doing?" Zandra asked.

"It was touch and go for a while, but the doctor got his magic stable," Verity said. "Of course, he has to serve his time for what he did to Nahla, but given the extenuating circumstances—the fact she kept him a prisoner in their marriage by drugging him—it's likely he'll only serve half his sentence."

"You're still in contact with Ivan?" I asked.

"He's a charming man. I didn't think it was serious between us, but we're still dating."

"That must be tricky while he's inside," Zandra said.

"Love comes with challenges." Verity smiled. "And I've been meaning to say, as a thank you, I want to offer you tea and scones for life."

"That sounds good." There was a note of caution in Zandra's voice. "Just make sure there are no weird herbs or enchanted honey in the scones."

Verity's cheeks flushed. "I'm so embarrassed that I got caught up in that ridiculous situation. I should have known something strange was happening when people kept coming back and bulk ordering food. I thought they loved my scones, not that my produce was tainted."

"Your scones are delicious," I said. "And as you said, business is booming, so you have nothing to worry about."

"I've learned my lesson," Verity said.

"How's your new hire working out?" I nodded at Reeny, a small, industrious house-elf, who'd gotten himself trapped in a slave contract with a family of messed up mushroom peddlers. That elf had been a serious thorn in my side while solving a recent murder, but no one deserved to be trapped as a penniless slave. So after some nifty negotiation and mild threats to his owner, I'd figured out an alternative. One that ensured Reeny kept his nose clean and his fingers busy.

"Oh! He's wonderful." Verity's smile was genuine. "Reeny is so polite and helpful. I was happy to offer him a job. Please, stop by anytime you want for a treat and you can catch up with Reeny. I've got a festive afternoon tea special, with sweet trimmings. Marshmallows included."

"We're working on a case at the moment," I said, "but I'm sure we can make time. Perhaps Tempest would like to join us."

"That's your sister?" Verity looked at Zandra.

"Yep. Tempest and Wiggles are here for the holidays."

"They've been in my tearoom twice! That little hound ate ten scones in one sitting."

"And he's about to demolish that enormous plate of marshmallows," I said. "This competition is over before it's started, thanks to greedy guts."

Verity grabbed a sand timer. "I'm in charge, so I'd better go. Good luck to your sister."

"She'll need it pitched against Wiggles," I said.

Verity counted everyone down, then flipped over the timer, and the fun began. Marshmallows were stuffed into mouths as the crowd cheered them on. Wiggles huffed out a small flame and partially melted his plate of marshmallows then inhaled half the gooey stack in one go, his cheeks bulging as he chewed and his tail thumping with joy.

After five minutes of chomping on marshmallows, two of the contestants bowed out. One of them looked green. Tempest and Wiggles were still going. Another contestant groaned, put their hand over their mouth, and dashed out of the tearoom, merry laughter following them.

Wiggles raised a paw. "More marshmallows!"

"What's the prize?" Zandra asked.

Verity, still standing close to us, said, "A gourmet basket of chocolate and cake. The second Wiggles saw it, he entered himself and Tempest. He's a determined little guy, isn't he?"

"He's as stubborn as they come," I said. "Especially when there's a basket of treats with his name on it."

Surprisingly, Tempest's plate had emptied quicker than I thought it would, and she was on her second large mound, almost keeping up with Wiggles. Something small, black, and furry darted out of Tempest's jacket, taking several marshmallows before disappearing.

I chuckled to myself. She still had those kittens with her, and they were helping to ensure a Crypt witch win. It was cheating, but Tempest got points for ingenuity.

The final contestants bowed out, pushing back from their marshmallow-strewn plates and shaking their heads.

Tempest glanced at Wiggles and nodded. She raised a hand, indicating she was finished, but her mouth was so full of marshmallows, it was impossible to hear what she said.

Verity stepped forward, a big smile on her face. "Wiggles is the winner!"

Wiggles leapt onto the table, blasting smoke into the air as he wagged his tail excitedly, his cheeks still bulging with gooey delights.

The prize was awarded, and it was such an enormous basket of treats that it dwarfed my furry friend, so I understood Wiggles' desire to win. We joined them as the crowd slowly dispersed and settled at a table.

"How's the investigation going?" Tempest wiped marshmallow from the corners of her mouth and downed a glass of water.

"We're learning these angels come with a giant side order of dodgy," I said. "We're supposed to be interviewing Nisroc, but he hasn't shown up yet."

"They're never as pure as they like everyone to think." Tempest pointed a thumb at the prize. "We can eat some of this later. You'll be back at Vorana's for dinner?"

"We wouldn't miss it," I said. "And Vorana will be pleased she doesn't have to make dessert."

Tempest nodded her head toward the door. "Is that your missing angel walking past the tearoom?"

"That's Tabris," I said. "We should nab him while we have the chance."

We said goodbye to Tempest and Wiggles, who were investigating their prize, then dashed out into the snow, calling after Tabris.

He turned and smiled, giving a small bow. "Ladies. How may I be of service?"

"You're due to be interviewed by us later," Zandra said, "but we may as well do it now."

"Here? It's rather chilly for a cordial conversation."

"We can keep it informal for now. Let's take it back to the tearoom, shall we? Do you like scones?"

Tabris glanced away. "If it's not inconvenient, I wanted to browse the excellent bookstore you have in town."

"That suits us," Zandra said. "We know the owner."

We fell into step with Tabris. He was tall and broad-shouldered and had a wonderfully calm aura. He had a deep timbre to his voice, and it soothed me as he spoke. It had an almost hypnotic quality.

"Despite the tragedy, I am enjoying my time here," Tabris said. "It's my first visit to Crimson Cove, and it's a most exhilarating town."

"We like living here," I said.

"I can see why. Any town with such a wonderful bookstore would always be at the top of my list of places to visit."

"What do you like to read?"

"Anything spiritual that speaks to the soul," Tabris said. "The others tease me that I'm the group pacifist."

"Is that true?" Zandra asked.

"I have been known to diffuse an argument or two."

We reached the bookstore, which had a beautiful display of festive decorations in the window, thoughtfully designed by Vorana, framing festive reads her customers might enjoy.

"Who's been arguing in your group?" I asked.

"Not so much our group." Tabris stopped and inhaled deeply as we entered the store. "There is nothing more pleasant than the smell of a bookstore. Shall we browse while we talk?"

"So long as you don't mind people overhearing our conversation," Zandra said. "We want to talk to you about what happened with Habriel."

"Of course. I have no secrets, so I'm happy to discuss anything." Tabris drifted along the book stacks, while Zandra waved a greeting at Vorana, who was busy with customers. He stopped in the spiritual section and browsed.

"You've known Habriel since your Academy days?" Zandra asked.

"That's right. We joined at the same time."

"What was your friendship like?"

"Habriel was the group's entertainer." Tabris pulled out a book and read the blurb on the back. "A showman, so entering the music industry made sense."

"Did he like to be the center of attention?"

"Some people do, and he was one of them. I appreciated that. I like a quiet life."

"Working at Angel Force can't always be quiet," I said. "Not when you're dealing with criminals."

"I'm not in active law enforcement." Tabris placed the book back on the shelf. "I run the healing and counseling service we offer to all angels. As you can imagine, it's a stressful job, and as you rightly pointed out, dealing with people who find themselves on the wrong side of the law is stressful. Sometimes, our angels witness terrible things, and they need something to soothe their souls. That's where my team comes in."

Tabris's calming tone was so relaxing, it almost lulled me to sleep. He'd chosen the perfect career path.

"Did you ever counsel Habriel?" Zandra asked.

"No, but I'll be honest with you. Even if I had, there is little I could tell you. Client files are confidential. Of course, you could get access to them with the appropriate warrant, but you'd find nothing about Habriel. He had a healthy degree of confidence, and he only worked at Angel Force for a short time before he left."

"Being famous must come with its own stresses, though," I said.

"I imagine so, but Habriel took it in his stride." Tabris edged along the book stack.

"Were there people in your group of friends he didn't get along with?" I asked.

Tabris studied the back of a book for a long time before answering. "Habriel liked pressing buttons for fun. He enjoyed seeing people's reactions when he stirred them up."

"That doesn't sound pleasant," I said. "Did he do that to you?"

"A time or two, but by then, I was deeply immersed in developing my counseling skills, so if I grew agitated, I leaned into my meditation and deep breathing. It works wonders. Perhaps you should try it." He glanced at Zandra's shoulders. "You're carrying tension."

"Investigating a murder will do that to a person." Zandra shrugged. "What were you doing on the night of Habriel's murder?"

"I was at the party, the same as everybody else," Tabris said. "In fact, I got there early. I greeted everyone, and we spent the evening enjoying each other's company."

"Did you see anyone confront Habriel at the party?" Zandra asked.

Tabris pursed his lips. "There was a small disagreement with Nisroc. I spoke to him for several minutes after it happened to ensure he was calm. Nisroc lives on his nerves, and Habriel always knew how to rile him."

"What was the argument about?" I asked.

"I didn't overhear their conversation, but I saw the end result. Habriel was laughing when Nisroc stormed off. I followed Nisroc to make sure he was okay, but he didn't want to talk about what they'd discussed."

"Does Nisroc have anger issues?" I asked.

Tabris stared off into space for a few seconds. "Nisroc is a good angel, and he does his best."

"That didn't answer my question."

"He's reliable and kind. But when someone doesn't respect that, it ruffles his feathers."

The more we learned about Nisroc, the more suspicious he seemed.

"Did Nisroc do or say anything that made you think he'd go after Habriel when the party ended?" I asked.

"Oh, nothing like that. As far as I know, Nisroc went to bed at the hotel at the same time as all of us. We were all there."

Just then, the bookstore door opened, and Sorush appeared. He raised a hand to Tabris in greeting, but when his gaze settled on us, his smile faded. Why wasn't this angel happy to see us? Was he concealing secrets, too?

I looked at Zandra. "Shall we? We may as well kill two angels with one stone."

# Chapter 12

## Super fan

Sorush turned away, intent on leaving the store. "I didn't realize you were busy. I'll find you later, Tabris."

I leapt off Zandra's shoulder and blocked the door, and she swiftly assisted. "Please, join us. You'll find the conversation interesting."

"I... I don't want to get in the way if you're busy." Alarm flashed in Sorush's startling blue eyes, and he tensed.

"We're due to meet later today, anyway," I said, "so this will save us both time, don't you think? Or don't you want to talk to us?"

"It's not that. Why wouldn't I want to talk to you? It's just that I'm... not prepared."

"What do you need to prepare for, exactly?" I narrowed my gaze. Sorush was panicking.

"It's just, well, Habriel was my best friend. I'm very emotional. I keep bursting into tears at the strangest things. I was watching children play in the snow, and before I knew it, I was blubbering.

I scared them! Angels aren't supposed to scare people."

"It's the shock." Tabris joined us by the door and rested a hand on Sorush's shoulder. "Death plays havoc with us. We think we have everything under control, but grief bursts through at the most inconvenient moments."

"You would know, since you're the expert," Sorush said. "I just wanted to feel strong enough before I was questioned."

"The questions aren't stressful," Tabris said. "I've just been having a pleasant chat with Zandra and Juno. They don't think any of us are involved, but they want to get to the bottom of things. We may be able to help them figure out what happened to Habriel."

Sorush sniffed. "You're right. I'm being foolish."

"Grief and sadness are never foolish," Tabris said.

Sorush looked down at me. "Let's get it over with. Although I'd like it if Tabris stayed."

"I have no problem with that." I looked at Zandra, and she nodded. "Let's find a quiet corner in the bookstore, and you can tell us all about Habriel."

Sorush looked tearful as we found a space at the back of the bookstore and settled into comfy armchairs. "I could talk about Habriel for hours. We were close. When he wasn't busy touring or working in the studio, we spent all our time together."

Tabris made soothing noises as he sat in his own seat.

"It must be hard to lose someone you're that close to," I said.

"Yes, it's a big void that no one else will ever fill."

"Did you share a love of making music?" Zandra asked.

"I haven't got a musical bone in my body," Sorush said. "I was even asked to leave the Academy's choir because I couldn't hit the right notes."

"What did you have in common with Habriel, since music was his biggest passion?" I asked.

"His enthusiasm for life!" Sorush brought out a mobile snow globe and scrolled through it for a few seconds before passing it our way. "We spent time together at his concerts and the after-parties. The venues were so full of energy and excited people. It was intoxicating."

I studied the photographs as Zandra flicked through them. Most of them were of Sorush and Habriel, standing together. Sorush was always beaming in the photographs, but Habriel often appeared bored or was looking away as if he wanted to be somewhere else. Were they best friends, or was Sorush more of an obsessed fan who wouldn't take a hint?

"It looks like you had plenty of adventures together," I said.

"Habriel always got me free tickets to his shows. Although I had to nudge him now and again to make sure he didn't forget his old friends. Not that he'd ever forget me." Sorush took back his mobile globe and slipped it into his pocket.

"Did you ever join them?" I asked Tabris.

"No, I found the shows too hectic. All the noise and overexcitement taxes the nervous system. If I ever listen to live music, it's in a small, intimate venue where you can see the musicians and enjoy the tunes without being crushed."

"It was always so incredible," Sorush said. "I've traveled all over the place to go to his gigs. Habriel always sold out. It was my hobby."

"You'll find a new hobby, my friend," Tabris said.

"Or perhaps you'll continue to follow Habriel's band," I said.

Sorush shook his head. "It won't be the same. Habriel knew the best places to go and the coolest people to hang out with. I don't think I'll bother going to the Christmas concert. Did you hear they're turning it into a memorial event?"

"I hadn't heard that," Tabris said. "It sounds like a suitable way to remember Habriel. Perhaps we should go. Out of respect."

Sorush tilted his head from side to side. "But Habriel won't be there. There'll be no celebrations afterward. He'd always invite groups of fans backstage so we could celebrate together. His parties got wild. And when his fans knew we were best friends, they were interested in getting to know me, too. I was a popular guy."

My impression of Sorush soured as he kept talking about the fan fun he had at the parties. Did he only remain friends with Habriel to gain access to overexcited concertgoers? Everyone knew what went on at a lot of show after-parties, and it concerned me that powerful angels had been exploiting that situation for their own gain.

"Perhaps there'll be an opportunity for us to have a private booth," Tabris said. "We could remember

Habriel together as a small group. I'm sure they'll play all of his favorite tunes."

Sorush's forehead furrowed. "It'll just be a bunch of miserable, crying fans. Where's the fun in that? No one will want to party."

"The fans adored Habriel as much as you did," I said. "Don't you want to reunite and remember your best friend?"

"No! I want to remember Habriel for the live wire he was."

"But you must enjoy his music since you went to all his concerts," Zandra said. "Don't you want to go for that?"

"I wasn't there for the music, just the vibes and the fun times. Although I left him a few reviews, so he'd know what a great friend I was. Not everyone is so generous with their words. Some supposed fans can be mean."

"We are truly sorry for your loss." I pushed as much sincerity into my voice as possible.

Sorush missed the sarcasm and nodded. "It's appreciated. I don't know what I'll do now he's gone. Are you any closer to finding out who did this?"

"We're still looking into things," I said. "We know for certain it was someone strong and powerful."

"And someone who hated Habriel," Zandra said. "We're thinking it must have been an angel."

Sorush and Tabris exchanged a startled look.

"I was unaware you were looking in our direction," Tabris said. "This is troubling. We would never hurt Habriel."

"We've learned Habriel wasn't as pure as his angel wings suggested," I said. "There have been mentions of him bullying other angels. Did either of you experience that?"

"That was a misunderstanding," Tabris said. "I mentioned he liked to press people's buttons, but that's different from bullying."

"Habriel wasn't a bully," Sorush said. "He could be tactless with his words, which annoyed people, but he meant nothing by it. He was just here for the good times. That's what I loved about him. He never took anything seriously."

That most likely included his alleged close friendship with Sorush.

"Could an uninvited guest have slipped into our party?" Tabris suggested. "It was a busy evening, and there were a lot of angels there. We stuck to our private area, but maybe someone got in who shouldn't have."

"Are you thinking of anyone in particular?" I asked. "Perhaps someone with a grudge against Habriel."

"I have a theory." Sorush's expression was serious. "Habriel had the most perfect voice. Almost as good as Virgil's."

"Your other friend? We've already spoken to him," I said. "I didn't realize he was in the music business, too."

"He's not," Sorush said. "But they sang together at the Academy. I never said it to Habriel, but I thought Virgil's voice was way better than his. Habriel even mentioned a time or two that he was jealous of Virgil's ability but then laughed it off."

"If Virgil was the better singer, why hasn't he pursued a singing career?" Zandra asked.

"It's not so much about the sound, but more about the charisma," Sorush said. "That's why I enjoyed spending time with Habriel. His aura attracted people to him."

"Do you mean women?" I asked.

"Sure. He got the hottest women. But he was always generous. Any he didn't have time to handle, he introduced to me. We'd end up going to his parties together and rocking out."

"What a convenient arrangement." Zandra's tone was flat, but annoyance burned in her gaze. She had the unsavory measure of this angel.

"Yes! For everyone." Sorush appeared oblivious to how awful he sounded. "We all had a great time, went to loads of parties, and had fun. Now it's over because someone messed with Habriel."

"Getting back to Virgil," Zandra said, "you mentioned Habriel was destined for fame rather than Virgil. Are you suggesting Virgil killed Habriel because he was jealous? Or that he arranged for someone to sneak into town and freeze him?"

"No! I mean... I don't know what I'm saying. I knew I shouldn't say anything. I'm not prepared. I told them I wasn't prepared." Sorush grew flustered until Tabris took his hand.

"Take deep breaths. Give yourself time to think. You know you say things you shouldn't when you get stressed."

"This is what happens when I'm unprepared. I panic and say dumb things." Sorush did deep breathing for a minute.

"So, Habriel and Virgil?" I asked. "Virgil didn't like how famous Habriel was?"

"Habriel was one of a kind. He only had to walk into a room, and everyone stopped to look at him. Virgil is just... Virgil. He's a nice guy, but there's nothing special about him," Sorush said.

"Not his incredible voice?" I asked.

"Oh, sure. That's amazing. Every time he sings, the hairs on my arms stand up, but then you hang out with him and he's just... I don't know how to say it without sounding rude." He looked at Tabris.

"Virgil has a decent heart and can always be relied upon," Tabris said. "But he's a little dull. Since he lost his chance to progress in music, he became obsessed with celestial magic."

Sorush cast his gaze at the ceiling and sighed. "He can talk about celestial magic for hours. It's boring. He gets giddy and obsessed about it and is always going on about a new spell he's tried or an old incantation he's discovered in some dusty book. Who cares? That kind of knowledge won't get the girls, will it?"

"It might appeal to a certain kind of lady, but they most likely don't go to pop-rock concerts," I said. "Did Virgil hold any resentment toward Habriel because he eclipsed him?"

"There must've been some jealousy there," Sorush said. "Habriel was popular with everybody. All our Academy tutors wanted him to do his best, and our music tutor pushed him hard. She had contacts in the business, so she got him an introduction, and off he went. He did his two years of designated service, which we all have to do once we finish at the Academy, and then he was out of there."

"And Virgil wasn't gifted that opportunity?" Zandra asked.

"If he asked for an introduction, he didn't get it," Sorush said. "And it makes sense. Virgil doesn't have any star quality. Unless that star is bland and cold."

This was an interesting turn of events. Virgil had the skills to freeze Habriel to death, and now he had a motive. If he'd wanted a music career and Habriel had gotten the spot because of his charisma and his way with the ladies, it must have left its mark.

"Since you brought up Virgil's name, do you think he's involved in the murder?" Zandra asked.

Sorush huffed out a breath. "I wish I'd never opened my mouth."

"But you did," I said. "Do you think he did it?"

Sorush glanced at Tabris. "We were all together."

"At the party?"

"Yes. At the party. All of us. All night."

"You must have spent most of your time with Habriel, since you were such good friends."

"We hung out, but he was generous and liked to share his time with everybody," Sorush said. "He was a good guy like that."

"And when did you leave the party?" I asked.

"Around midnight, with everyone else. Habriel hit me hard with a snowball when we were messing around outside. It left a bruise."

"We all threw a few snowballs that night," Tabris said. "We'd enjoyed a lot to drink and were merry with the season."

Sorush had revealed himself to be an unpleasant angel and perhaps more of a fanboy than a best friend to our victim, but I couldn't uncover a motive for wanting Habriel dead. Could Habriel have rejected Sorush's friendship? If he had, Sorush appeared oblivious to subtleties, so he most likely hadn't noticed. And to complicate things, he'd shoved Virgil into the limelight and then backed off. What was this angel up to?

"I hope you find whoever did this," Sorush said.

"We have every intention of doing so," I said.

"Have either of you seen Nisroc?" Zandra asked.

Tabris's forehead furrowed. "He was at the hotel this morning."

"He didn't show up for his interview with us."

"He's around. If I see him, I'll remind him," Tabris said. "He's usually so reliable."

We thanked them for their time and said our goodbyes.

"Take out your snow globe," I said to Zandra.

She pulled it out. "What are we looking for?"

"It was something Sorush said about reviews and mean fans. Find some reviews of Habriel's band."

Zandra was immediately scrolling on her mobile snow globe. There were pages and pages of reviews on Habriel's music. Some of the fans raved about it, while others were lukewarm. There were even one-star reviews and comments about it being generic and unoriginal.

"Look at that! It's the same guy posting one-star reviews on all of Habriel's music," Zandra said. "And on all the sites. It must have taken hours to write these and post them everywhere. This name keeps coming up. Listen to this: 'Habriel's talent is as mediocre as his looks. He's usually too wasted to hold a note and always uses auto-tune. Don't believe it when he tells you he writes his own lyrics—he has a team behind him. The guy is a fraud. And remember, looks fade. Talent lasts forever. We'll soon know the truth.' That's how it ends."

"And it's written by V.I. Angel," I said.

"Could that be Virgil?" Zandra asked.

"V.I. Angel. Would he be so stupid to do that? It won't be hard to track these back to him," I said.

"Why would Virgil write mean reviews if he was friendly with Habriel?" Zandra asked.

"Maybe they were never friends. Habriel pressed Virgil's buttons at the party," I said. "Dredged up old memories and made him remember everything he lost because of Habriel's oh-so-cool charisma."

"Which is why Sorush blabbed to us. The guy has no filter. They must have been gossiping about Virgil killing Habriel," Zandra said.

"Virgil somehow got out of the hotel, caught Habriel as he was sneaking off with the stolen books, and blasted him with celestial magic," I said. "Since we can't find Nisroc, let's question Virgil again and see what he has to say about Habriel's star shining too brightly for him to bear."

# Chapter 13

## Truth unfurls

After everything we'd learned, we were now hunting for Nisroc and Virgil. Nisroc's disappearing act was suspicious, but Virgil had lied about his relationship with Habriel. He wanted what Habriel had, and perhaps he thought that, with him dead, he stood a chance at the fame that had been denied him.

"Let's refuel before we carry on." I shook snow out of my fur. "We have time, since Bertoli is running a trace to find out if Virgil is behind all those spiteful one-star reviews."

"We're spoiled for choice with the Christmas market." Zandra stopped to inspect a stall selling handmade candles. "What are you in the mood for? Sweet or savory?"

"I'd usually say fish, but since it's almost Christmas, we should stick to the festive treats."

"More pigs in blankets?"

"Now, we're talking."

We spent a few minutes investigating options before settling on turkey loaded nachos with a side order of extra turkey for me. The snow was coming down harder as we got close to the center of town, where the decorated tree and remaining ice sculptures were placed. There was a large crowd ahead of us, and as we grew closer, carols began.

"I forgot they were doing a carol service in town," Zandra said.

We stopped for a few minutes, eating our food and enjoying the ever-so-slightly off-key tunes. The singers started with a traditional festive carol and then moved on to a more modern number.

"I'm sure that's Wiggles howling along to the music." Zandra grinned.

After a moment of searching the crowd, I spotted Wiggles standing next to Tempest, his head back as he howled at the cloudy sky. We continued walking around the edge of the crowd toward them, then I slowed. Virgil was there with several other angels. He saw me looking at him and turned away.

"That's Virgil!" I was already bounding across the snow, still chewing on my last mouthful of turkey, with Zandra close behind me.

By the time we reached the small group of angels, Virgil had gone. He was heading away from the crowd and not being slow about it.

"What's got him in such a hurry?" Zandra scooped me up and settled me on her shoulder so I didn't have to dash through the snow as we continued following Virgil.

"It could be that Tabris or Sorush tipped him off that they'd been gossiping and dropped him in it. They could have felt guilty that they'd gotten their friend into trouble and wanted to give him a heads-up."

Virgil glanced over his shoulder, speeding up when he saw we were following.

"That angel definitely doesn't want to talk to us," Zandra said.

"Let's see if we can change his mind." I cast a spell that whacked him in the behind, causing him to yelp.

He spun around. "What did you do that for?"

"We needed your attention," I said. "Where are you going in such a rush?"

"Nowhere. I mean, it's cold, and it's snowing. I wanted to get in somewhere warmer."

"You seemed happy enough to stay with your friends and listen to the carols until you saw us," I said.

"I... I didn't see you. Why would I be looking for you? I don't know you."

"The second you saw us in the crowd, you left," Zandra said. "Tell us why."

"It's a coincidence! I really should go." He turned away.

I lashed out with a murder mitten and attached it to Virgil's wing, causing him to freeze. "We've been hearing interesting things about your singing ability. Apparently, you have an even better voice than Habriel."

"I... Could you remove your claws from my wing?"

"Will you run off if I do?"

"I wasn't running!"

Zandra arched an eyebrow, and I twitched an ear.

Virgil sighed. "Can we at least take this somewhere inside, where it's not freezing? The hotel is only a few minutes' walk from here."

"No flying off," Zandra said. "We will follow you. And if you run, what will that make us think?"

Virgil gulped. "Sorry. I panicked. I know you're asking questions about what happened to Habriel. Please, I've done nothing wrong. But I really am cold."

I released his wing, and we hurried to the Sleepy Stardust Sanctuary, the snow pelting down with an icy malevolence. Lizzie served us hot drinks and sugar cookies before leaving us in the small guest sitting room.

"You and Habriel sang in the Academy choir, didn't you?" I settled against Zandra's belly to warm up.

Virgil looked puzzled as he nodded. "That's right. Why are you interested in our old choir?"

"Because we've heard you weren't happy he was the favored singer, especially considering your voice was better than his."

"The quality of singing voices is always subjective," Virgil said. "Some people prefer my voice. Some prefer Habriel's. What does that have to do with anything?"

"You must have been jealous that Habriel was favored by the Academy tutors," I said. "There you were, also an excellent singer, yet they ignored you because of your lack of star quality"

Virgil took a few seconds to sip his drink as a dull flush rose up his neck and onto his cheeks. "Our Academy days were a long time ago. I barely remember them. There's no point in living in the past, is there?"

"But you are," Zandra said. "You've been leaving bad reviews on Habriel's music."

The flush on his cheeks deepened. "No, I haven't!"

"We made the connection ourselves," I said. "V.I. Angel. You could have picked a more discreet username. Or did you want Habriel to know you were disrespecting his career?"

"Who told you this?"

"We got talking to Tabris and Sorush, and Angel Force is checking the data to confirm our suspicions, so there's no point hiding it. Your friends mentioned how unhappy you'd been that Habriel got the glory, even though you were considered the better singer. How did they describe Virgil?" I glanced up at Zandra.

"Lacking in star quality," she said. "Average."

Virgil thumped down his mug. "We're supposed to stick together. Why would they tell you that?"

"Because they're worried you may have done something bad to Habriel," I said. "You told us you lost contact with him over the years and that your friendship drifted. But when we looked at the reviews, it seemed you never had a friendship. You were intensely jealous of Habriel's success and took delight in writing terrible reviews of his music."

"I'm an honest angel," Virgil said. "If someone produces substandard work, I let them know."

"You're admitting you wrote those negative reviews under that username?" Zandra asked.

Virgil's eyes narrowed. Then he sighed. "It was unfair. My music tutor at the Academy told me I had the best voice they'd heard in over a century. There isn't a note I can't hit. But did that matter when Habriel auditioned for the choir? He didn't even prepare, but they were entranced by him. Everyone who met him fell under his spell."

"Because he had that elusive star quality," I said. "Impossible to define, but some people just have it."

Virgil's top lip curled. "Star quality! I should have been the famous one. Habriel joined the choir because of a bet. He didn't even want to do it, but when the Academy tutors fawned over him and told him how amazing he was, he stuck with it."

"And you got left behind, seething with jealousy," I said.

"I didn't seethe," Virgil said. "I still enjoy music, but I focused on another career. My work with Angel Force is rewarding."

"But you could have had so much more," Zandra said. "The glittering stardom Habriel obtained."

"And look where that got him," Virgil said. "It was grossly unfair. He coasted along and got everything without making any effort. I worked so hard in that choir, and it was as if I didn't exist."

"Which sounds like a solid motive for murdering him," I said.

Virgil tensed in his seat. "Hands up, I didn't like the guy. His charisma came across to me as arrogance. But I didn't want him dead. Besides, I was at the party, along with everybody else. I couldn't have killed him."

"You could have snuck off once you were back here," I said.

"I didn't! I enjoyed myself with my old Academy friends, and that was it. Yes, there was some envy stirred up when I saw Habriel and witnessed the effect he had on everybody, but I'm no killer. I couldn't have done it. I was here!"

And that was the problem. Virgil, along with everyone else, had the same alibi.

"I got my revenge with my reviews," Virgil said. "And they were honest. Habriel did use auto-tune. I've never needed that. I'm note perfect."

"We could ask everyone at the party if they saw you leave the hotel," Zandra said.

"Do it. There was no sneaking off anywhere that night. I went to bed, and I didn't stir after my head hit the pillow."

"And at the party, were there no comfort breaks? Trips to the bar? Did you dance at any point during the evening?" I asked. "It would have given you a chance to scope out the best way to kill Habriel when no one was looking."

"We had our own private bathroom and a small dance floor, so we didn't have to leave our private area. The drinks were brought to us, unless we wanted something special. Although Nisroc kept buying everyone shots. That treatment is a perk of being in the top ten percent of graduates from the Academy. They look after you, even once you've left." Virgil shifted in his seat. "You can ask anyone at the party or anyone I went to the Academy with. I'm no killer."

"But you have an obsession with celestial magic," I said.

"Which I openly revealed to you," Virgil said. "Yes, I have the ability to freeze someone, but why do that when it would make me the obvious suspect? Surely, I'd use another method to kill. Angels aren't supposed to kill, but we have the ability to do so in plenty of ways."

Virgil made some good points, and although he'd initially appeared flustered when we started questioning him, he was now more relaxed.

"What about Nisroc?" I asked.

Virgil tilted his head. "What do you want to know about him?"

"Did he have any issues with Habriel?"

He drew in a breath. "What have you been told?"

"We heard from a reliable source that Habriel was a bully. In particular, he picked on Nisroc. Is that true?" Zandra asked.

"Habriel could be a jerk, especially to Nisroc," Virgil said, his tone now soft. "And Nisroc is odd. He's always been on the outside of the group. When we joined the Academy, we made an effort to include him, but it was as if he didn't function well in a crowd. He'd withdraw and stop speaking. Get him on his own and he's fine, but he has serious social anxiety. Unfortunately, Habriel noticed and was quick to make fun of him."

"Did you do anything to stop that?" Zandra asked.

"Of course! I told Habriel not to mess with Nisroc, but he never listened. Habriel was far too self-important to listen to reason. And when the tutors got obsessed with him and guided him toward stardom, he only got worse. That was when I backed away. I was glad when we graduated because it gave me a reason to cut ties."

"Do you think Nisroc wanted revenge?" I asked. "Seeing Habriel again must have stirred up painful memories. Memories he acted upon."

Virgil looked doubtful. "As I said, Nisroc doesn't open up easily. Habriel could be hard on him, so there must have been some resentment there."

"When was the last time you saw Nisroc?" I asked.

"Earlier today, at the hotel, I think," Virgil said.

"He missed his interview slot with us," Zandra said. "The next time you see him, send him our way."

"Missed his interview? That's not like Nisroc. He's quirky but reliable. If he says he'll be somewhere or do something at a certain time, he always does it." Virgil's forehead furrowed. "You don't think... Well, you're asking about Nisroc's issues with Habriel. You don't think he's the killer, do you?"

"We think we need to have a conversation with him," I said. "Unless there's something you want to tell us?"

"No! No. I don't know what happened to Habriel. I had my issues with the guy, but to be frozen to death like that is cruel."

"Just like Habriel could be to Nisroc," I said.

"Yes, perhaps so. But Nisroc being involved with this murder. I... I don't know. Then again, I lost touch with him once we left the Academy. Nisroc spends most of his time alone. He prefers it that way."

"Make sure you don't leave town," I said. "We could have more questions for you."

"We're staying for the rest of the holidays. And I'll help in any way I can." Virgil hurried off to his room in the hotel, and I sat in silence with Zandra as she finished the cookies, and we mulled over the information.

"This has to be the most unreliable group of feathers we've ever had to deal with," Zandra said. "They all have their issues, or they're hiding something from us. How are we supposed to solve Habriel's murder if they don't tell the truth?"

I tensed as the atmosphere sparked with power.

"What the..." Zandra jerked out of her seat, her hands flexed as she sensed the shift in energy surrounding us.

A second later, an icy, sugar-scented swirl wrapped around us, and two sparkling hands appeared and yanked us into it.

# Chapter 14

## Higher surprise

"What in the name of all things frosty is going on?" Zandra yelped as we were tossed head over tail repeatedly through the cinnamon sugar-scented swirl.

"Higher angels," I hissed as I somersaulted through the air. "They must want to talk to us."

"Then send a freaking message like any normal person!" Zandra flipped over again and almost crashed into me.

The sugary swirl ended abruptly, and we landed in a pile of freezing snow. Except it wasn't freezing. It was sticky, like marshmallows. We'd landed in a giant pile of partially melted marshmallows. At least, that's what it felt like.

Zandra groaned. "I feel queasy."

"Welcome to our magical winter wonderland." Ted stood by the edge of the giant pile of marshmallow-like substance. "We wanted to surprise you."

"You managed it." I made sure my wonderful witch was unharmed before plowing through the sticky substance and rolling out of it.

"Don't you like it?" Ted's beaming smile faded. "We don't have weather here. Not like you do in Crimson Cove, so we did our best to replicate snow and ice. We wanted to make it festive, but not freezing. I do not enjoy the cold. It's horribly numbing to the extremities."

Tinkerbell strolled into view, her tail up in greeting. "I warned them this wasn't a solid plan, but they didn't want actual snow, so settled on marshmallow snow instead."

"So I'm gathering." I flicked a piece of gooey sludge off my paw. "Why are we here?"

Bilious floated into view, his feet several inches off the ground. "Welcome to our magical winter wonderland."

"I've already done that," Ted said. "We should have had a tree. I told you they wouldn't be happy unless we had a tree with lights and sparkle, like the one in the middle of the town. A tree would have made this perfect."

"No tree and no snow. None of that is necessary," I said. "But we would appreciate an explanation. As you're aware, we're in the middle of a murder investigation."

"We are indeed aware, my finest magical creature," Ted said. "Which is why you are here. We intend to have festive fun and find out exactly what happened to dearest... what was his name again?"

"Nisroc. You've been investigating the murder, too?" Zandra attempted to scrape marshmallow snow off her jacket.

"No! That's what you're doing. But first, I insist upon a snowball fight!" Ted grabbed a giant handful of marshmallow goo and slung it. It hit Zandra squarely on the forehead, and she fell back into the gooey sludge with an oomph.

I hissed a warning. "Be careful!"

"Oh, my. Sorry! I forget my own strength when dealing with lower beings. She's not dead, is she?"

"If my witch was dead, you would be, too," I said.

Zandra was sitting up, rubbing her forehead. "Give me some warning the next time you want to knock me out. It'll give me a chance to fight back."

"With thousands of apologies, tiny witch. If I'd known you were so feeble, I'd have hurled a smaller ball." Ted appeared suitably sorry, his wings drooping and his sparkle less sparkly.

"We should have the festive fun after we've discussed the murder," I suggested. "That is why we're here, isn't it?"

"Yes! Among other things," Ted said. "Tinkerbell, did we make a final decision on the food?"

"I said hot chocolate and some of that disgusting fruitcake covered in icing and marzipan would do."

"Of course, you remarkable creature. Bilious, fetch the refreshments. We must ensure our guests' desire for Christmas treats is fulfilled."

"There's no need for treats," I said. "And we must get back to Crimson Cove. There's lots to do."

"All in good time. In fact, we can compress time for you. You'll be back there, and only five minutes will have passed."

"That would be convenient," I admitted.

Bilious returned, pushing a trolley that had what looked like an enormous wedding cake on it. There was a small witch and a white cat perched on the cake's top tier.

"Wow! That's quite some cake," Zandra said. "Did you make it?"

"I tried, but something caught fire. Tinkerbell made the arrangements. There's hot chocolate, too." Bilious lifted a pitcher of sludgy brown liquid and poured it all over the cake.

"No! It's not pouring chocolate. It's drinking chocolate." Tinkerbell shook her head and licked a paw.

"I forget! People do so many strange things with chocolate. Do you drink it? Eat it? I've even seen soap that smells like it. What do you do with that? Eat it and then clean your armpits with it? The world beneath us is bewildering."

"Try a piece of cake. Even with the chocolate on it, I'm sure it'll be delicious." Ted cut two enormous chunks of cake with a sparkling blade that he'd slid out from under his white robe. There were no plates, so he dumped my piece of cake in front of me and insisted Zandra hold out both hands to receive hers.

"I'm more of a savory fan," I said.

"I told you we should have gotten something special for Juno," Ted said to Bilious. "She eats like Tinkerbell. Roast chicken and butter fried salmon."

"It's good cake," Zandra said. "Kind of weird tasting but edible."

"There are pixie shavings in there," Bilious said. "I had to go to three markets to find it. Those didn't catch on fire, so I added them to the icing."

Zandra discreetly spat the cake into her hand and held it behind her back.

The higher angels looked at us expectantly.

"Are we still on the festive fun, or do you want to hear about our progress with the investigation?" I asked.

"We can do both. But let's focus on the murder," Ted said, suddenly all serious. "Who is your prime suspect? I learned that term by watching television dramas. There's always a prime suspect. And it's never who you think. There's a twist in the tale. Imagine that. What if there was a twist in this tale? It would almost be fun."

"Murder is rarely fun," I said, "but the suspects can be sneaky. And they are in this particular investigation."

"Tell us of their sneakiness," Bilious said.

I exchanged a look of exasperation with Zandra, but we wouldn't be getting out of here until we'd shared. "We questioned Bertoli first, since he was a graduate at the same time as the other angels. We couldn't find a strong motive for him, and he was at the party all evening."

"They all were," Zandra said. "And that's the problem we keep coming up against."

"Don't spoil the ending," Bilious said. "Who else are you considering?"

Zandra lifted her shoulders. "Virgil. He has an interest in celestial magic and the ability to freeze another angel."

"That's an impressive power," Ted said. "But he can't have done it."

"Why do you say that?" I asked.

Ted splayed his fingers. "Well, he's an angel."

"It may have escaped your attention, but all of our suspects are angels," I said. "You need to suspend your disbelief if we're to make progress."

"Oh! Of course. Yes. All angels. Please, go on."

"We discovered Virgil hated Habriel," I said. "He's been following Habriel's career and discrediting him by writing negative reviews about his music. And, it turns out Virgil has the better singing voice, but because of Habriel's star quality, Virgil was overlooked when he was a student."

"Which made him jealous of Habriel's success," Zandra said.

"How distasteful," Bilious said. "His alibi?"

"At the party, along with all the other angels," Zandra said calmly. "And then they went back to the same hotel as a group. Habriel was renting a house. And Bertoli went to his own apartment."

"Yes! You said that. About the party. And then they all went home together." Bilious nodded along at his own summary.

"Not Bertoli," Zandra said.

"He has no motive, though."

"Right. And Habriel was alone, too."

"But he didn't do this to himself, so who's next?"

"Arioch. He claimed to be on friendly terms with Habriel," I said. "They'd inspire each other to be the best versions of themselves."

"That sounds like a healthy relationship," Ted said. "There's no reason for Arioch to want Habriel dead. Let's move on."

"Before we do," I said, "when we questioned Arioch, we discovered he uses gray magic."

Ted and Bilious inhaled sharply and reached out to clasp hands.

"We followed Arioch and discovered he was using gray magic to save an old tutor who'd gotten herself in trouble. He's not turned rogue."

"This is most alarming," Ted said. "Did you arrest him?"

"No, although he has a possible motive, even though he denies it. Perhaps Habriel discovered Arioch was dabbling in gray magic and thought it would be fun to ruin his reputation," I said.

"And his alibi?" Bilious asked.

"Have you forgotten what I told you?" Zandra tutted. "All the angels were at the party all night. None of them left. Then they all went back to the same hotel. Apart from Bertoli and Habriel."

Ted and Bilious exchanged perplexed looks, as if this was the first time they were hearing this information.

I checked in with Tinkerbell, and she simply shrugged. Living with the higher angels, she must be used to this quirkiness.

"We've also spoken to Tabris, who doesn't appear to have a motive. And Sorush. He claimed to be Habriel's best friend, but it was easy to see their close friendship was anything but. Sorush exploited Habriel's fame so he could get tickets to his concerts, including the after-parties, where there were lots of available starry-eyed women to have fun with."

"That doesn't seem like the behavior of a respectable angel," Ted said. "Are you sure any of that is true?"

"We're sure. He told us himself," Zandra said. "He couldn't resist bragging about getting the women Habriel was too busy to handle. It was gross."

"Is that everybody?" Ted asked. "No devils? Strange snow beasts? Anyone other than an angel as a suspect? I'm concerned you're only focused on angels. And we don't kill."

I inhaled. "Our prime suspect—"

Ted squeaked and clapped his hands together in a show of joy.

"Is Nisroc," I continued. "Several of the other angels have mentioned his name and said he stood out at the Academy for the wrong reasons."

"He's also missing," Zandra said. "He didn't show up for his interview, and he hasn't been seen since this morning."

Ted raised his hands, suggesting he was about to make an announcement. "This calls for a game of Reindeer Rings."

"Not the rings. Can't we play Butthead?" Bilious asked.

"Is now really the time for games?" I asked.

"I'm kind of interested in seeing what Butthead involves," Zandra murmured, a half-smile on her face.

"Oh! Yes! Butthead. We must play Butthead. Bilious wears the hat, and you throw the balls. That way, you won't be knocked senseless." Ted dashed away before anyone could stop him and returned with a hat covered in sticky strips, which he strapped onto Bilious. Then he handed Zandra half a dozen soft foam balls. "Throw those as hard as you can. Bilious dodges to avoid getting covered in the balls."

I looked at Tinkerbell, who shook her head and yawned. "Don't even try to stop this. They get so excited about Christmas. They've been alive for centuries, yet they never tire when this time of year rolls around."

Zandra was more than happy to lob balls at Bilious while he raced about, laughing like a deranged fairy who'd just snorted a kilo of pure glitter.

"Do you really think an angel is the killer?" Tinkerbell had sidled over to me, and we sat together while watching the chaos.

"From what we've learned, none of the angels are perfect. They're all hiding secrets."

"Having spent time with the higher angels, I've discovered they're anything but angelic," Tinkerbell murmured. "It's a given that any magical being that stays alive for so long gets warped. That truth trickles down to the regular angels, too. They may once have been pure of intent and action, but these days, they're as messed up as the rest of us."

"Does that mean you're not enjoying your time living with Bilious and Ted?"

Tinkerbell gave me the catlike version of a smile. "I've never been happier. They're insane, eccentric, and have lost touch with reality, but I'm never bored. They brush me for at least an hour every day and hand-feed me morsels whenever I demand it. You should hook up with an angel if you ever get bored with Zandra."

"I'll never tire of my wonderful witch, nor she of me," I said. "And you're right about the regular angels. They're messy."

"I got him!" Zandra bounced up and down as Bilious admitted defeat, his head covered in the balls.

"Now the fun is over, you might like to see the background check I ran on Nisroc," Tinkerbell said, lifting a paw as a sheet of paper floated down and landed at her feet.

"You're so clever!" Ted picked up Tinkerbell and smothered her in kisses until she whacked him hard on the nose with a paw.

I read the report. "It's from Nisroc's Academy days. There's mention of horseplay."

"Oh! Horseplay." Bilious's expression dropped. "How dreadful. Let me see."

I stepped back as he flipped a pair of bizarre-looking glasses over his eyes, held out a hand, and blasted light onto the paper, the beam scanning the words. "Yes, it is true. This sad specimen of an angel struggled. Nothing came easy to Nisroc. Such a pity."

"Even so, I can't believe he turned to darkness," Ted said.

"According to some of his friends, Nisroc argued with Habriel at the party," I said. "The pair had issues."

"But not murderous issues, surely. Give me a moment to access the Academy's records," Bilious said.

I was going to ask if they had a computer, but all he did was press two fingers against the side of his temple and close his eyes. Another surge of light shot into him, and he swayed back and forth.

"Don't get freaked out by the light show," Tinkerbell said. "This is how they do things around here. You have the Internet, and we have the Angel Web. It's basically the same thing, but the information is transferred into the higher angel's brain. I think it's one of the reasons they're so peculiar."

Bilious's eyes snapped open, and he removed the glasses. "Horseplay at the Academy, too."

"Which translates into bullying," Zandra said. "Was it between Habriel and Nisroc?"

"Sadly, yes," Bilious said. "Habriel targeted others as well. He was a high-spirited young angel."

"Which means a nasty jerk," I said. "Virgil said Habriel had an ego that got too big as his star was buffed for fame."

"We should visit the Academy," Zandra said. "Speak to the staff. They could know something that never made it into the records. Something sketchy that meant Nisroc would murder Habriel when an opportunity showed up."

"No, as I said, it can't be our angels," Bilious insisted. "Perhaps a stranger. Or a snowman?"

"Oh! The snowman! I forgot. Bring it in." Ted floated several inches off the ground. "Bring it in this instant. How could I forget our finest festive treat for our guests?"

"What's happening now?" I asked Tinkerbell.

"Just go with it," she said. "If you expect the unexpected, you're rarely terrified."

Another giant cake was wheeled in by an invisible hand, and before it even stopped moving, a huge snowman blasted out of the center. An actual snowman. He was made of snow, had two coals for eyes, and a carrot for a nose. He danced around us, seemingly without any direction, content to shimmy and sway to a tune only he heard. At one point, he tried gyrating on Zandra. He lost his nose.

"What fun," Bilious said. "Isn't he fun?"

"He's... something." Zandra shoved the raunchy snowman away. "Who should we contact at the Academy?"

"Don't bother the Academy," Ted said. "They're busy. You should go with our snowman theory. Don't you see how strong they are?"

Zandra kicked the snowman as he twerked in front of her. "Real snowmen don't do this!"

"And a snowman didn't murder Habriel," I said.

"How do you know? They can become enchanted," Ted said. "What about an errant reindeer? This time of year, they're ghastly. It's their mating season. All the bucks want to impress their ladies."

"Reindeers mate in springtime. We're focusing on the angels closest to Habriel," I said. "I offer our sincere thanks for this most entertaining time in your realm but request you send us home. If we're not in Crimson Cove, we'll never be able to solve the murder."

"Wait!" Bilious raised a hand, light glowing from him. "I have a hint of Nisroc. Just a tiny pinprick."

"Why so tiny?" Ted whispered. "Don't tell me our beloved angel is concealing himself from us?"

"If he killed Habriel, he'll stay in hiding," I said. "Is he in Crimson Cove?"

"I believe so." Bilious swayed alarmingly fast. "I'll send you back there now."

Before I had time to take a breath or say goodbye to Tinkerbell, an icy cinnamon swirl wrapped around us. We were flipped head over tail so many times I lost count and then dumped onto freezing ground.

I rolled over in dry leaves to find Zandra next to me, sucking in deep breaths. "I wish they'd give us a warning before doing that. I don't do rollercoasters, and that was twice as sucky as any rollercoaster."

I looked around. "I thought they said they'd compress time. When we left Crimson Cove, it was just getting dark, but the moon is now high. It's the middle of the night!"

"Typical higher angels. They have no concept of day or night." Zandra stood on shaky knees. "Where did they dump us?"

"In the middle of Crimson Cove woods," I said. "Is this where Nisroc is hiding?"

While Zandra straightened her clothing, muttering to herself about how irritating higher angels were, I picked up a distinctly angelic scent. But it was faint. Barely discernible.

I lifted my booping snooter and took a few steps forward. Peering over a fallen log, I discovered Nisroc's frozen body on the ground.

# Chapter 15

## Frosty the frozen

Zandra had joined me by the log, and we stared down at Nisroc in silence. He was long past saving.

"This complicates things," she said. "Our prime suspect is dead!"

"I wonder for how long?" I carefully sniffed the frozen corpse. He'd been frozen in the same way as Habriel, although the expression on his face was one of fear, not surprise. Total and utter horror.

"Nisroc missed his interview with us." Zandra was crouched, looking around the scene. She shivered. "He could have died the night before."

"Some of his friends saw him in the morning," I said. "Why would he have come into the woods on his own?"

"They said he was a loner," Zandra said. "Maybe he found the hectic Christmas chaos too much and needed time with nature."

"And the killer followed him and struck," I said.

Zandra shivered again, glancing up as snow pelted through the tops of the trees. "We can't stay out here for much longer, or we'll end up just like Nisroc."

"Having Wiggles around right now would be handy. He's always free with his fireballs," I said. "I'll see what I can muster up."

"Don't melt Nisroc!" Zandra said. "We don't want to miss any clues."

"There could be a clue right in front of us, and we'd miss it because it's so dark." I hovered a small fireball over our heads, creating an eerie, shadowy surrounding that did nothing to cheer up this sad scene.

"Nisroc has his hands up, as if he tried to ward off whoever did this to him," Zandra said. "Unless..."

"What are you thinking?"

"He messed up and did it to himself? Wracked with grief over killing Habriel, he turned the powerful magic inward."

"If Nisroc decided to end things, why aren't his hands pressed against his own chest?" I asked. "And the frozen look on his face suggests he knew what was coming for him but couldn't get away in time to stop it."

"Does that mean we have a serial ice killer on our hands?" Zandra asked. "Someone is targeting this group of angels and freezing them as a punishment?"

"Punishment for what? Something to do with what happened at the Academy when they were students?"

"Or something they did after they graduated?" Zandra suggested. "And I'm not necessarily thinking something bad. They could have brought down a criminal, and now he's out and on the loose, looking for revenge."

"If they were all in active law enforcement, that would be a possibility," I said. "But Habriel only stuck around for the minimum amount of time, and Tabris provides therapy and counseling. He's never arrested anybody."

"So, our fearsome, frosty fiend is one of the angels we're already focused on," Zandra said. "Did Nisroc kill Habriel, and one of his friends got revenge?"

"Virgil has the skills to do this. He figured out what Nisroc did, so he gave him a taste of his own icy medicine. But we still come back to the problem of how the first murder took place," I said. "The angels on our suspect list were at the party and then went to the hotel as a group. It was only ever Habriel who was on his own that night."

"And Bertoli."

I sighed. That was true, but I didn't have it in me to see Bertoli as a killer. He could be a grump, but he was a law-abiding grump. "If Nisroc iced Habriel, how did he do it without any of his friends finding out?"

"This is proof he was seen. Another angel saw Nisroc sneaking out of the hotel, followed him, and watched as he froze Habriel. Then they waited until the right moment to get their revenge." Zandra briskly rubbed her arms as the snow grew fiercer. "But whatever happened here, we won't figure it out by standing here getting numb toes."

"I agree. It's too dark to see anything useful. Let's mark this spot and take Nisroc to Sorcha's freezer. We'll keep him with Habriel. We can better inspect his body there, and we'll return to the woods in the morning when it'll be easier to see what happened."

Decision made, we swiftly translocated Nisroc into the café's freezer. After we'd settled him next to Habriel, we left the freezer. There was raucous laughter in the café and music playing.

"It must be a vampire evening," I said as we headed into the café.

The place was full of Remus' vampires. He was holding court, telling some amusing tale, with a glass of what looked like red wine in his hand, but we both knew it wasn't. Sorcha stood behind the counter, shaking her head and smiling as she prepared a platter of food. Her eyebrows rose when she saw us.

"Hey! Did you just come out of my freezer again?"

"Yes, we found another body," Zandra said. "We had to stash him before he melted."

She blinked rapidly in surprise. "Who is it this time?"

"Another angel," I said. "Nisroc. He was frozen, just like Habriel. I hope it won't spoil the party, us showing up with such an unwelcome gift."

"My most magnificent witch and my delightful furry friend!" Remus swooped over and embraced both of us. "Although no invitation was issued, you're welcome at my gatherings. I brought my hive here to enjoy some early festive fun. Sorcha hosts the most wonderful intimate gatherings."

"You celebrate Christmas?" Zandra asked.

"I enjoy any excuse for a party," Remus said. "And did I just overhear another frosty body has shown up?"

"Yes, but keep that information to yourself for now," I said. "Cythera doesn't know."

"You two look frozen through," Sorcha said. "I've got hot toddies on the go if you want something to help you warm up. I make them with blood, but I can sub that for something you'd like."

"That sounds perfect," Zandra said. "My nose is numb."

While Sorcha made our drinks and delivered a tasty plate of festive nibbles, Remus leaned against the counter. "I'm glad you're here. I still feel dreadful about my hive's recent bad behavior."

"That's in the past," I said around a mouthful of salmon. "No one was behaving like themselves."

"Yes, those pesky mushrooms have a lot to answer for," Remus said. "But we've paid the appropriate amount of compensation to anyone we nibbled upon. And you'll be happy to hear, no one was turned, and everyone is much restored. I even hosted a champagne gala for anyone who'd been bothered by my vampires during that trying time. The turnout was splendid. It ended in a naked conga around the grounds."

"Where was our invitation?" I asked.

Remus ducked his head. "I was concerned you'd turn me down. My hive behaved dreadfully, as did I, and Archie thinks you despise him. He remembers how unkind he was to you. He whimpers about it every night before we go for our moonlight wanders."

"I'm still friends with Archie," I said. "I hold no grudges. He might be interested to meet Wiggles. He's a miniature hellhound, turned by magic.

His power is extraordinary, so they'd have fun together."

"Archie is always delighted to make a new friend, so I'll let him know," Remus said. "And thank you for your kind words. Not many would be so benevolent, given how uncouth I was."

"We're just happy to see everyone back to normal." Zandra was smiling at Sorcha's boyfriend, Denver, as he helped behind the counter with a tray of warm blood bottles.

Remus looked on with a satisfied smile. "All these frozen angel bodies are most intriguing, though. I always knew the angels had a dark side."

"As we're finding out," I said. "The suspects are slippery, the opportunity is tricky, and the motive is murky."

"Don't tell me there's a case that's bested you, my delicious fluffy fancy?"

"I'll never be defeated when there's an injustice waiting to be resolved," I said.

"If I hear anyone bragging about their use of ice magic, I'll send them your way, shall I?" Remus asked.

"All help is welcome," I said.

Remus returned to the party, and after warming up with hot drinks and food, we said goodbye to everyone and magicked home.

Tomorrow, we had to tackle two murders with no decent suspects.

I rolled over and twitched my booping snooter. There was an odd scent in the basement. I opened an eye and squeaked. Cythera loomed over the bed.

Zandra grunted. "Go back to sleep. It's too early."

"We have a visitor," I said. "Greetings, Cythera. Were we expecting you?"

Wiggles lifted his head. He grumbled several times and nudged Tempest until she roused.

Tempest's expression was groggy as she stared with unfocused eyes at Cythera. "It's way too early for this. We'll leave you to it." She rolled off the bed, scooped Wiggles up, and they headed upstairs without saying another word.

"Send down coffee," Zandra called after her.

"How can you be sleeping when another angel is dead?" Cythera's wings flared.

"How do you know about that?" I asked.

Zandra rolled onto her back and sighed. "One guess. Remus is terrible at keeping secrets. That vampire is such a gossip."

"It doesn't matter where the information came from. You should have told me immediately."

"In case you've forgotten, we're in charge of this investigation," I said. "What would you have done if we'd pestered you in the middle of the night and told you another angel had died?"

"Demanded answers!"

"Which you're not permitted to do. When we found Nisroc, it was late, snowing hard, and there was no sign of his attacker in the woods," I said. "We did the best we could in difficult circumstances. We looked for obvious evidence then safely transported Nisroc to the freezer. He spent the night with Habriel. Now it's light, we can go back to the woods and search the ground again."

"How did you know where he was?" Cythera asked.

"We were visiting Ted and Bilious. They got a hunch about Nisroc's location."

"They called it a ping," Zandra said.

"Oh! Yes, a ping on his location."

"How? Why were you with them?" Cythera's expression tightened.

"They dragged us into their realm for a weird Christmas party. There was a gyrating snowman and a cake with pixie shavings." I smoothed some ruffled fur back into place. "You know what the higher angels are like. They click their fingers, and there you are in another dimension."

"You must show me Nisroc's body," Cythera said. "I insist on being involved. You've done nothing to progress this case, so I'm taking over."

It began to snow in the basement.

"Uh-oh. The higher angels must be listening to our conversation, and they're not happy," I said. "You know you can't be involved in this case."

"Bad Cythera," Zandra said. "We'll get on the investigation as soon as we've woken up, you've stopped hassling us, and we've eaten breakfast."

I smirked at my witch's sassy tone. You should never bother Zandra before she was caffeinated. "Now, off you go. You're only slowing us down by being here and demanding things we can't give you."

Her wings twitched. "This is outrageous!"

"It is also your reality," I said.

Cythera turned and stomped up the basement steps. A few seconds later, Vorana called out a greeting to her, which was met by a door slamming.

"We'd better get a wriggle on," I said. "Cythera will be on our backs until we figure things out."

After Zandra had used the bathroom and gotten dressed, we headed upstairs. Vorana, Tempest, Wiggles, and Sage were in the kitchen, already eating breakfast.

"Cythera didn't spend the night, did she?" Vorana asked when she saw us.

"She gave us an unwelcome wake-up call," I said. "It was terrifying."

"And after finding another body last night, we deserved a lie-in," Zandra said. "That won't happen now."

Vorana's eyes widened. "Another body?"

"You didn't tell them?" Zandra asked Tempest, who'd been given a full run down when we'd gotten home, before we'd crashed for the night.

"Nope. I rarely talk much before my second pot of coffee."

We filled Vorana and Sage in on the latest over a plate of cranberry-iced muffins and big mugs of coffee.

"So you have two victims. What about your suspects?" Vorana asked.

"Nisroc was our prime suspect for murdering Habriel. He was bullied and an outcast, so it was obvious he was involved," Zandra said.

"But now he's dead," I added.

"Is Bertoli still on your suspect list?" Vorana asked.

"We only interviewed him to get a rise out of Cythera," I said. "It's possible he was on the receiving end of Habriel's bullying, too, but I don't see him as a killer."

"Are you looking for one killer or two?" Tempest asked.

"We're uncertain at this stage," I said. "One of the angels, Virgil, can freeze people. He was jealous of Habriel's success, but I'm unsure why he'd want Nisroc dead."

"Is there anyone else?" Vorana asked.

"Arioch uses gray magic, and we wondered if Habriel had learned about it and was blackmailing him, but again, why kill Nisroc?" Zandra said. "The same goes for Tabris and Sorush. They all basically ignored Nisroc. He was on the outside of the group."

"Perhaps he tried to change that, but something went wrong," Vorana said. "He knew who murdered Habriel and decided to spill the beans. The killer would have had to silence him."

"Didn't you say the suspects were at the party we went to?" Tempest asked. "If they were there, none of them could have killed Habriel, could they?"

"That's the problem we've yet to get around," I said.

Zandra finished her coffee. "If we can figure out who murdered Nisroc, we may be able to link Habriel's murder to them, too."

"You've got a lying angel," Tempest said. "If they're prepared to lie, they're prepared to do other nasty things to hide their secret. Watch your backs out there."

"You could watch them for us." It would be useful to have another powerful Crypt witch and her fire-breathing companion on hand if the angels turned evil.

"No can do." Tempest wiped crumbs off her fingers. "We're doing a sleigh ride today and then spending the afternoon in the teashop."

"The festive high tea is not to be missed," Vorana said. "I've been in twice. So much yummy food."

I finished my salmon. "You have fun, but after breakfast, we're outing our lying angel and plucking them until they confess."

# Chapter 16

## Angel odd

Our first stop was the crime scene where we'd discovered Nisroc's body. It was no less frosty, but at least we could see more clearly. I had my fur fluffed out to its fullest to keep warm. Zandra was wrapped in a scarf with a woolen hat jammed low on her head as we surveyed the scene for any clues to help us discover who froze Nisroc.

We walked in a circuit and then in straight lines, but nothing revealed itself. Not so much as a rogue angel feather that had fallen from the killer's wing as he made his escape.

"Whichever angel did this could have flown in and out," I said. "Or even hovered in the air and blasted Nisroc, not needing to touch the ground."

"Nisroc must have trusted whoever lured him into these woods," Zandra said. "You don't go out on a night like that for something insignificant."

"Let's assume Nisroc knew what happened to Habriel," I said. "He must have been torn between revealing all and keeping his alumni buddy's secret. Perhaps Nisroc wanted to meet Habriel's attacker to find out why they did it or to give them a chance to confess. He had to choose a meeting place somewhere discreet where no one would see them."

"Which means we're still looking at one of the other angels," Zandra said.

"We need to figure out what they were all doing at the time of Nisroc's murder."

"Several of his friends reported seeing him at the hotel the morning he was supposed to meet us to be interviewed, so it must have happened after that."

"That still leaves us with a big window of opportunity," I said. "Let's stop at the hotel and check with Lizzie to see when she last saw Nisroc. That may help. Then we need to go to the freezer and see if there's anything useful on the ice body."

"And then we're back to questioning what's left of the alumni angels."

A visit to the Sleepy Stardust Sanctuary revealed Lizzie had barely seen Nisroc. The only times she could confirm seeing him were during check-in and after the group returned from the party.

We walked to Sorcha's café, and after spending a few minutes examining Nisroc, we found nothing of use. There were no signs of any injuries inflicted before the ice spell hit him. And unless he'd made a run for it, there wouldn't be. Nisroc had been caught just like Habriel, with nowhere to escape.

Sorcha was busy behind the counter, so we left her to it and headed outside into a crisp and frosty morning.

My gaze landed on feathers and a blaze of dazzling white. "Let's try some shock tactics."

"Who are we shocking?" Zandra rubbed her hands together.

"Sorush and Tabris have just come out of the apothecary. If they're innocent, they won't know what happened to Nisroc. We'll watch their reactions when we reveal the truth to see if they have anything to hide."

Zandra nodded, and we hurried over to the two angels, who were deep in conversation.

"We're so sorry for your loss," I said.

Sorush stopped walking and looked down at me. "Thank you. We're adjusting to life without Habriel."

"I didn't mean Habriel. I meant Nisroc," I said. "You must have heard what happened to him."

The angels exchanged puzzled glances.

"What's happened?" Tabris asked. "I was beginning to think Nisroc had left town, since I hadn't seen him for such a long time. He didn't show up at breakfast."

"He won't be showing up for any more meals," I said. "We found Nisroc frozen to death in the woods, just like Habriel."

Sorush gasped, and Tabris exhaled sharply. Both of their shocked expressions appeared genuine.

"Did anyone see what happened?" Tabris was the first to recover.

"Not that we know of," I said, "but we're investigating."

Sorush fluttered his wings. "Could it have been a guilt freeze?"

"Could you elaborate?" I asked.

"I'm sure your investigation has revealed Nisroc wasn't the most popular in our group," Sorush said. "We liked him, but he had some strange ways about him."

Tabris nodded, looking sincere. "He couldn't overcome his shyness. He struggled in group situations, and we were always doing things as a big group. That meant he either didn't show up, or he lingered in the background, looking uncomfortable. That made it uncomfortable for everybody else. It was a delicate situation to manage."

"Because Nisroc had social anxiety, you mistreated him?" I asked.

"No! Well, I never did," Sorush said quickly.

"But Habriel was another story?" Zandra asked. "He was the bully."

"Habriel couldn't understand why Nisroc was so quiet," Tabris said. "He teased him. Perhaps Nisroc had enough. The party brought everything back to him, and he taught Habriel a lesson."

Sorush nodded along. "And then, caught up in his grief, he turned the magic on himself. Nisroc would have been weighed down with guilt over what he'd done."

I shook my head. "Given the evidence we found, it's almost impossible that happened."

"What evidence do you have?" Tabris asked. "I thought you didn't see what happened to Nisroc?"

"We're working on some theories," I said.

They waited for more information, but they weren't getting help from us.

"It's a sad day, losing two of our old friends so close together," Tabris said.

"I have a great idea," Sorush said. "We should offer to speak at Habriel's service. Angel Force will host something elaborate to remember him by, and we'll need to be there."

"Will you speak at Nisroc's service, too?" I asked.

Sorush pulled a face. "If the angels insist upon it, but Nisroc wasn't famous, so his service won't pull an exclusive crowd. I doubt there'll be many mourners going to it."

"I heard a rumor that Habriel's service will take place just after Christmas," Tabris said. "He always enjoyed this holiday, so they can have a wintery theme at his final farewell."

"The date doesn't matter," Sorush said. "We'll be available over the holidays."

"Don't you have families you want to spend time with?" I asked. "Partners or wives?"

"Sorush is committed to the life of a single bachelor. He has no one to kiss under the mistletoe," Tabris said.

Sorush shoved him. "Yeah, good one. I have plenty of ladies interested in me."

Tabris tilted his head. "Is that so? When was the last time you went on a date? You know my door is always open when you need to discuss your inability to form a lasting bond."

"Why do you keep trying to dig around in my personal life?"

"Because you don't have one. And we all know why." Tabris waggled his eyebrows. "It sometimes needs more than time to heal old wounds."

"Don't spout your meditation clap trap at me!"

"It's not clap trap. It's grounded in science. And magic."

"We don't know why," Zandra said. "Why don't you tell us?"

"My personal life has got nothing to do with anyone," Sorush said. "Some of us don't brag about our accomplishments with the ladies."

From what had come out of Sorush's mouth since he arrived in Crimson Cove, that wasn't true.

"Habriel bragged about his conquests, didn't he?" I asked.

"He was a chronic over sharer," Tabris said. "We learned to block out the noise."

"Nisroc didn't approve, though," Sorush said. "He never said anything, but you could tell by the look in his eyes that he hated when Habriel disrespected women. It's another reason he'd want to end our friend's life and then turn the magic on himself. This is a valid theory. We should suggest it to Cythera. She'll make sense of this mess."

"Cythera's not working this case," I said. "No angel is impartial enough to be involved."

"If we were, the mystery would have been solved by now," Sorush said.

"But would that solution have been correct?" I asked.

"My friend means no offense, and I'm sure your skills are excellent, but we are unique," Tabris said. "And we wouldn't have wasted time questioning innocent angels when there's an unhinged maniac out there freezing us." Sorush jabbed a finger.

"You just suggested Nisroc was involved, though," I said. "If we hadn't interviewed any of you, we would have missed him as a suspect. Or are you aware who this mysterious, unhinged maniac is?"

"Oh! Well, what I meant was, we wouldn't have wasted time interviewing anyone but Nisroc," Sorush said. "What is it they say about keeping a close eye on the quiet ones? That was our mistake with Nisroc. He must have been inside his head all the times he sat outside the group, not taking part or having fun. He did that to himself. He can't blame us."

"He can't blame anyone for anything, since he's dead," I said.

"Maybe he was quiet because he was trying to figure out why his friends ignored him?" Zandra suggested.

Sorush bristled. "Are you saying, if we'd been kinder to Nisroc, Habriel would still be alive?"

"Nisroc and Habriel," Zandra said. "Because Nisroc froze himself to death because he was racked with guilt. That's the story you're telling us, isn't it?"

"No! No story. We're just making suggestions. Trying to be helpful." Tabris caught hold of Sorush's arm. "Everyone just wants to get along. Whenever there were problems in the group, I smoothed things over, so Nisroc was never too badly treated."

"You're good at smoothing things over. More like hiding things." Sorush pulled his arm away, still clearly annoyed at Tabris teasing him over being single.

"What do you mean by that?" Tabris asked.

Sorush gave another impressive display of finger jabbing. "I know you hid something during your interview."

"What did Tabris hide?" I asked.

"Sorush is teasing, and it's not funny," Tabris said. "This is a serious situation. Honesty is always the best policy when friends are dying."

"You should tell them. They'll be fascinated by your particular interests. Or is that part of your life smoothed over so no one notices you're not perfect?"

"I have no particular interests." A muscle flickered in Tabris's jaw. "We should leave. We're going to be late."

"You can spare us a few more minutes to tell the whole story." I blocked their path.

Tabris forced a laugh. "Really, it's nothing. Sorush has a terrible sense of humor."

"Just like me being forever single is nothing, right?" Sorush snapped. "I'd rather be happily single than part of a freak show."

What the snowy heck? Whatever these two were bickering about, we only had half the story.

"You only hate it because I'm happy," Tabris said. "I've explained the situation so many times, but you refuse to listen."

"What situation? What's going on?" Zandra asked.

Tabris glanced our way. "This is a private matter, and I can assure you it has nothing to do with what happened to Habriel or Nisroc. We're sure Nisroc was involved in Habriel's murder. Focus your attention there, not on my friend's poorly timed attempt at comedy."

Sorush glared at Tabris for a few seconds before nodding. "We've known them both for a long time, and I agree. Nisroc snapped. Habriel could be an idiot."

"And Nisroc was vulnerable. It made for a toxic situation," Tabris said.

"Let's assume you're right," I said. "Habriel pushed Nisroc too far, so he acted. But what happened to Nisroc? He died in the same way as Habriel. Who did that to him? It wasn't self-inflicted, and there are few people who could pull off such an intense spell on such a powerful individual."

They exchanged a wary glance.

"Go on, we're interested in your theories," I said. "As you said, you've known each other a long time. Who is most likely to have killed Nisroc?"

"Virgil has the ability," Sorush said after a short pause. "But it couldn't be him."

"I agree. This is hard for me to say, but what about... Bertoli?" Tabris asked.

"Why bring his name into the mix?" Zandra asked.

"He shares certain similarities to Nisroc," Tabris said, a note of hesitancy in his voice. "Although I can't go into the details, he has used my services, so I know he's troubled."

"Bertoli is in therapy?" I asked.

"He had stress-related issues not so long ago," Tabris said. "In fact, thinking about his case, you were mentioned. Juno and Zandra. Yes! It's coming back to me now. You were the cause of his stress. How remarkable."

I hid a smile. Early on in our relationship, things had been tense. Bertoli had been a little uptight, and I'd been a little less than generous with my patience. It hadn't helped that the first time we met, he'd accused Zandra and me of beheading someone.

"I like Bertoli, but he is strange. Go pester him," Sorush said.

"We'll be talking to you all again to find out what happened to Nisroc," I said, still befuddled by their sudden finger-pointing toward Bertoli. "Remind us when you both last saw Nisroc."

"Um... it was the morning he disappeared," Sorush said. "Right?"

"Yes. We were at the hotel, having a late breakfast. He wanted to spend time on his own—"

"No change there," Sorush muttered.

"So, we left him to it," Tabris continued. "We all left the hotel around eleven."

"Tell us where you were between the hours of noon and the early hours of this morning. Tabris, we'll start with you," I said.

"I spent time in town with the others. We all went out as a group to browse the market."

"The others being..."

"Sorush. Virgil. Arioch etc. All of us. Then we arranged to have pre-Christmas drinks and enjoy an evening of reminiscing about old times at the Academy."

Sorush nodded. "My day was much the same. We got together around five, drank, ate, and talked about what life was like before it got so complicated."

"Those were the good old days," Tabris said.

Once again, the angels were together when Nisroc had found himself in trouble. How unhelpful.

"Make sure you don't leave town," Zandra said. "We will get to the bottom of this."

"We have no plans to go anywhere." Tabris's smile was benevolent. "Bertoli is hosting us this year over the holidays. He makes an excellent nut roast."

"You're having Christmas Day at Bertoli's apartment?" I asked.

"We take turns hosting every year," Sorush said. "I just hope he doesn't make us play party games again."

"I enjoy the games," Tabris said.

Sorush shrugged. "I guess. And now Habriel isn't here, we'll all get a turn."

"Every cloud has a silver lining," I said. "Enjoy the rest of your day."

As we walked away from Sorush and Tabris, I hopped onto Zandra's shoulder. "We missed something in that conversation. They started out jokey but soon started snapping at each other."

Zandra nodded. "Sorush got teased for being eternally single, but Tabris has a secret, too. Something the other angels consider freaky. Maybe he's dating a demon."

"The way this case is going, I wouldn't be surprised if that's what we uncover next."

# Chapter 17

## Food fun

"Bertoli's not here." Cythera moved papers from one side of her desk to the other.

"Is he off investigating a case?" I hopped onto her desk.

She shooed me away. "Despite Christmas being a chaotic time, and I need all my angels here, he requested time off."

"Bertoli rarely takes time off," I said. "The only time he's been away was when he had his sergeant's training and the mandated anger management course he was forced to attend."

"Bertoli never used to be angry," Cythera said. "But when you and Zandra showed up, you made him twitchy."

"You can't blame that on us." I glanced at Zandra, who was lurking in the doorway. "Well, only partly. Anything could have triggered Bertoli."

"It was you. I'm blaming you," Cythera said. "If you must talk to him, he's at home. He's hosting his friends over Christmas and has been using every spare minute to make the food."

"Bertoli cooks? This we have to see." I was already heading out of the office.

"Don't be a pest," Cythera yelled after me.

"I'm never a pest, always a welcome addition to any situation."

We left Angel Force and marched briskly through the snow to keep ourselves warm.

"This'll be fun," I said. "Although Tabris mentioned something about a nut roast, so I hope it's not all plant-based. I have no aversion to people following that way of life, but there'll always be a space in my heart for a juicy plate of salmon."

"And burgers," Zandra added. "Also cheese."

"I doubt Bertoli will be making festive burgers, but you never know."

"There they are! Hey. Wait for us!"

I turned to find Sorush and Tabris hurrying toward us. We waited until they arrived, their faces bright pink from the cold.

"Have you been following us?" Zandra asked.

"No, but after our conversation, we got talking," Tabris said.

"What did you talk about?" I asked.

The angels exchanged a series of stressed glances. Neither of them seemed eager to speak.

"It's cold, and we've just had word of a festive feast awaiting us, so please don't delay any longer than necessary," I said. "Have you remembered something about the night of the party? Or a clue that could help us figure out what happened to Nisroc?"

"We don't like to tell on a dear friend," Tabris said hesitantly, "but... well, Bertoli didn't join us last night for drinks. He was supposed to, but he made an excuse."

"You said you were all there," Zandra said.

"We didn't want to get him in trouble," Sorush said. "And there's something else you need to know about him."

"Go on," I urged.

"At our private party, on the night Habriel died, Bertoli left. Not for long, but I saw him go out a back door. Ten minutes later, he returned."

"What time was this?" I asked. "After all, you left the party together, and Habriel was still alive."

"I'm not saying it had anything to do with what happened to Habriel," Sorush said, "but it was strange. I wondered if he was making plans to do... something."

"Plan a murder?" Zandra's brow furrowed.

"Perhaps Bertoli left the party to prepare the freeze spell," Tabris said. "He could create that magic when he was a student, but he found it draining. He may have needed extra ingredients to ensure its effectiveness. What if, and this is only a suggestion, he left the party to get those ingredients?"

"And Bertoli isn't staying at the hotel with us," Sorush said. "He was home alone."

"Why would Bertoli stay at the hotel, since he has his own place in town?" I asked.

"Exactly! I'm sure that's the only reason he didn't join us," Tabris said. "Nothing else. Maybe."

"You say nothing else, but you seem determined to plant the seed of doubt in our heads that Bertoli was involved with these murders," I said.

"We debated what to do," Tabris said. "We don't feel comfortable confiding our concerns about a friend. Bertoli is a reliable sort, but he can be odd. Just like Nisroc."

"We've worked with Bertoli ever since we moved to Crimson Cove," I said. "He has his faults, but do you really think your friend is involved in these murders?"

Sorush and Tabris looked bashful before they nodded.

"It feels wrong to keep these secrets from you when you're trying so hard to figure out what happened," Tabris said.

"And what if this killing spree isn't over?" Sorush asked. "First Habriel, now Nisroc. There could be someone targeting our group. They must be stopped."

"Why would they target you?" Zandra asked. "Does someone have a grudge against the friendship group? Have you received any threats?"

"No! We're friends with everyone," Tabris said. "We preach peace on earth."

"And goodwill to others?" I couldn't resist a little snark. I heard their words, but I wasn't sure I believed them. Why were they turning on Bertoli? Surely, they'd have revealed this information earlier if they considered it important. It was a significant clue, one that could lead to solving the murders.

I looked up at Zandra, and she shook her head, not seeming convinced either.

The angels seemed to realize there was doubt in our minds because they shuffled closer.

"It was wrong for us to hide this information from you," Tabris said. "And I'd never have considered Bertoli, but he was uptight when he was a student, and some things never change. I've offered him words of advice on how to manage stress, but he never took them. His life would be much happier if he didn't live in a swirl of stress all the time."

"Stress makes people do dreadful things," Sorush said sagely. "At least, that's what I've heard."

"Bertoli got so stressed that he killed two of his friends?" I asked. "I understand he may have had issues with Habriel. If Habriel was content to bully one friend, it's not a stretch of the imagination to think he did the same thing to Bertoli. But why would Bertoli turn on Nisroc? If Nisroc was on the outside of your special group too, surely they'd have bonded."

"Nisroc didn't do bonding," Sorush said. "And I don't know if you've noticed, but Bertoli doesn't have any friends. Apart from us."

"We're his friends," I said. "We look out for him. And friends accept each other's flaws."

"I suspect it's not so much friendship rather than sympathy you feel for Bertoli," Tabris said. "It's easy to mix those emotions. Bertoli is always so eager to please and follow the rules. That can be hard to be around."

"You're wrong. We're good friends with Bertoli," I said firmly. "And I find it impossible to believe he had anything to do with these murders."

"Ah! That could be a problem," Tabris murmured. "I didn't realize how close you were."

Zandra huffed out a breath. "Why is that a problem?"

"Perhaps it's you and your familiar who shouldn't be investigating this case. Your impartiality is tainted." Tabris raised a hand in a gesture of supplication. "You have a conflict of interest here, and we should inform the higher angels. Your friendship with a suspect will influence your final judgment in this case."

Zandra stepped forward, her hands clenched into fists. "If Bertoli had anything to do with either of these murders, he'll get what's coming to him. We don't let friendship get in the way of justice. Now, are there any more secrets you need to share, or can we get on and do our job?"

Both angels took a step back, the anger radiating off Zandra making it clear she wasn't prepared to be messed with anymore, not when it was so cold.

"I'm sure you'll do the right thing." Tabris's voice was laced with a patronizing lilt.

They turned and hurried away.

Zandra sneered at them. "What do you make of those two jerks?"

"They're suspicious," I said. "But we need to find out if Bertoli did leave the party. If that's true, he lied when we interviewed him."

Zandra scooped me out of the snow and placed me on her shoulder as we hurried toward Bertoli's home. "It can't be him. Sorush and Tabris are right. Bertoli follows the rules. It's painful to watch sometimes, but to turn on his friends and kill them, it wouldn't enter his head because it's breaking so many of the rules he loves to follow."

"I couldn't agree more. But let's start with the basics. We'll find out what he did when he left the alumni party and go from there."

Ten minutes later, Zandra was knocking on Bertoli's apartment door, having to move a large green and red wreath to one side to get to the knocker. Even though the door was closed, I got a whiff of delicious roasted meats.

It took thirty seconds, but Bertoli finally answered. He was dressed in a bright red apron and held a wooden spoon in one hand.

"I hope you're not planning on using that as a weapon against us." I gestured at the spoon with a paw.

He glanced at it. "I'm busy in the kitchen. What are you doing here?"

"We need to talk about your friends," Zandra said. "Mind if we come in?"

"Um... I guess not. But I can't leave the kitchen. I have multiple timers on the go."

"We're happy to talk while you cook," I said. "And whatever you're making smells divine."

A rare smile flashed onto Bertoli's face. "Thanks. I'm boiling a honeyed ham and have a lamb shank roasting. There are muffins and pecan tarts just out of the oven, too."

"Lead the way," I said.

Zandra stepped inside Bertoli's hallway, and we were met with a Christmas explosion. There was tinsel, holly, a tree in the corner flickering with lights, and a variety of stuffed festive animals that looked like they'd play a song if you squeezed their bellies.

"You really love Christmas," I said.

"It's my favorite holiday." Bertoli was already dashing back into the kitchen. "Cythera isn't keen on it because she thinks it makes people behave badly, but I love it. And I always see the opposite. People think about others. They reach out a helping hand and make connections with family they haven't spoken to all year." He glanced over his shoulder as we stayed in the doorway. "You've got family here at the moment, haven't you?"

"My sister, Tempest, and Wiggles," Zandra said.

"It's nice to catch up with family." Bertoli placed a muffin on a plate, covered it with icing and powdered sugar, and then stuck a small plastic sprig of holly on top. He handed it to Zandra. "Take a bite. Let me know what you think. Juno, would you like to try some ham?"

"I absolutely would."

"Give me a second to carve some off the edge. It's almost ready, but I'm giving it another ten minutes to make sure it's extra succulent for my guests."

"We heard you were hosting your friends at Christmas." I tried not to drool at all the delicious scents filling the kitchen.

He nodded as he placed several big chunks of steaming ham on a plate. "It needs to cool."

"This muffin is amazing," Zandra said, her words muffled by the huge bite she'd taken.

"I love baking," Bertoli said. "I used to do it when I was a kid. It brings back good memories."

"Yet you never bring treats into Angel Force." My gaze was fixed on the ham.

"I don't want the other angels to make fun of me," Bertoli said. "I have a professional image to uphold."

"Your image would only be enhanced if you brought in treats like this."

Bertoli cut the ham into smaller pieces, blew on them, and then passed some to me. "I don't know about that."

I was so entranced by the moist ham that I forgot the reason for our visit.

Bertoli cleared his throat as he watched us stuff our faces. "I'm guessing this visit is about Nisroc? Cythera told me what happened. It makes no sense. Why would anyone want to freeze him? The guy wouldn't say boo to a goose. He kept his head down and his mouth shut."

I gulped down three large chunks of glorious ham. "We've been talking to your friends, and they mentioned you and Nisroc were more like outsiders in the group. Is that true?"

Bertoli lowered his gaze. "We weren't considered the cool ones, if that's what you mean. It could be hard to fit in. I liked to study more than party."

"There's been a suggestion Nisroc attacked Habriel, and then, in a fit of grief, used the freeze spell on himself," I said. "Can you imagine he'd do such a thing?"

Bertoli's eyebrows shot up. "No! He'd never do that. Besides, I'm not even sure Nisroc could use that kind of magic. I remember him struggling with celestial spells. For some, it comes easy, but not for others."

"And for you?" Zandra asked.

Bertoli placed a slice of pecan pie on a plate and handed it to her. "Try this next. It's an old family recipe. I can use celestial magic, but it feels unnatural. I passed the tests, but it's not something I'd ever want to use again."

"Some of your friends are saying that's exactly what you did," I said.

Bertoli's expression grew puzzled. "You've lost me."

Zandra sighed and set aside the pie. "Fingers are pointing at you. Your friends think you were involved with both murders."

Bertoli's mouth dropped open. He took back the pie and what was left of the ham. "How dare you! You come here, eat my food, and then accuse me of a double murder?"

"Did you leave the alumni party?" I asked.

"I already told you I was there all evening with everybody else."

"So why have we been informed that you snuck out a back door?"

His eyes widened. "I... I didn't think anyone would notice me go."

"So you lied to us?"

Bertoli's cheeks flushed. "I didn't leave to do anything bad."

"What did you do?"

"I was running out of time. There was the party, work, all the food I had to get ready, and then I had to think about gifts. I realized I hadn't wrapped them."

"Gifts?" Zandra asked.

"Wait here." Bertoli dashed out of the kitchen, returning a few seconds later with two small wrapped parcels. "These are for you. I left the party because I saw you show up and remembered I hadn't wrapped up your presents. I knew I'd be busy hosting my friends and didn't want to forget them."

I looked up at Zandra in stunned silence. Bertoli had gotten us Christmas gifts?

"You didn't have to do this," Zandra said.

"I know everyone thinks I'm stuffy and uptight, but this is the one time of the year when I show people I have a different side. A fun side. A gift-giving side. Open them now if you like."

I ripped into mine and was thrilled to discover small packets of dried salmon and catnip mice. "What thoughtful gifts."

"They're only small things, but I hope you like them."

Zandra opened her gift to find some ground organic coffee and a thick slab of dark chocolate. "Thanks, Bertoli."

He leaned against the counter, glancing at the ham. "Maybe I haven't been entirely truthful when talking about my friends. Or rather, my lack of them. I didn't fit in with the other students. Habriel was over the top and unkind. He used to prank me. I don't think he meant it out of malice, though. Although there was this time I got locked in a closet for a day. I didn't enjoy that."

"And Nisroc?" I asked.

"Sure, he pranked Nisroc, too. But we moved on from that. And I'm as innocent as Nisroc. I'm sure he wasn't involved with what happened to Habriel.

And I don't believe for a second he'd freeze himself to death."

"Bertoli, you must understand why we have to question you," Zandra said. "You were the only one to go home on your own on the night of Habriel's death. And we've learned you didn't spend time with your friends on the day Nisroc was killed. They arranged an event, and you didn't show up."

"There was a gathering? I didn't know about that," Bertoli said. "Every spare second I have, I've been baking. I've been baking for days. Look in the fridge, and you'll see the truth."

Zandra opened the fridge to discover mountains of plastic boxes filled with food.

"These murders have nothing to do with me," Bertoli said. "I've barely had time to sleep, let alone commit two murders and hide the clues."

I looked at Zandra, and she shrugged. There was something going on here, but I couldn't figure out who was lying and who was telling the truth.

"Bertoli, do you know much about Sorush and Tabris's private lives?" I asked.

He pursed his lips and looked away.

"You do know something, don't you?" Zandra asked. "Go on, spill the beans. There's something going on between them, but they clammed up when we asked about it. They were making digs at each other. Could it have something to do with the murders?"

Bertoli frowned. "I doubt it. And it's private. I don't like to gossip about friends."

"They're gossiping about you," I said. "And any information could be helpful."

He sighed. "If I'm telling you this, we'll need coffee and much more cake."

# Chapter 18

## Tasty puzzle

Despite Bertoli snatching away the food, he couldn't resist showing off the delicious Christmas cake he'd made. He set it proudly in the middle of the table before cutting a generous slice for Zandra and himself while the coffee brewed. He also prepared me a small plate of fishy delicacies, for which I was most grateful.

With the refreshments ready and Bertoli finding no more reasons to stall talking to us, we sat at his table and waited for him to open up.

He stirred his coffee with vigor, keeping his gaze down. "How's the cake?"

"Excellent," Zandra said.

"And the fish?" he asked me.

"Delicious."

We waited some more.

"Let's start with Sorush, shall we?" I prompted. "Why did Tabris tease him about being single?"

"He has dated," Bertoli said after a long pause.

"But he doesn't anymore?" Zandra asked.

"He tries to, but he met his soulmate when he was young, and no one has ever measured up."

"There was no happy ending for Sorush and his soulmate?" I asked.

Bertoli shook his head.

Zandra lifted her chunk of cake. "Does Habriel have anything to do with Sorush being single?"

"Would you like more cake?" Bertoli asked Zandra.

"No. Just answer the questions," she said.

He sighed. "Sorush met Milandra just after graduation. The connection was obvious, and they were devoted to each other."

"So what went wrong?" Bertoli's evasiveness was infuriating me.

"Sorush made a mistake. He was trying to impress Milandra, so he took her to one of Habriel's shows. It was just after his band made it to the top, and their music was being played everywhere. Sorush got them backstage passes so they could meet the band and party."

"Let me guess. Milandra met Habriel and was star struck?" I asked.

Bertoli pressed his lips together as he nodded. "Habriel said he didn't know Sorush was serious about her. And he was quick to point out that if Milandra truly loved Sorush, she wouldn't have considered doing anything with another guy. Naturally, Sorush was heartbroken. They tried to make a go of things, but he couldn't move past the betrayal. Six months later, they separated, while Habriel pretended nothing had happened. By then, he'd probably gone through a dozen more women and forgotten about Milandra."

"Sorush found no one to replace Milandra?" Zandra asked.

"She was the love of his life." Bertoli sipped his coffee. "Sorush pretends it doesn't bother him, but you can tell he still thinks about her."

"Why did he remain friends with Habriel after that happened?" I asked.

"Because friends stick together," Bertoli said. "We were all in the same class and shared the same dorm at the Academy. That was our motto—through thick and thin, it didn't matter. We always looked out for each other."

"Habriel wasn't looking out for Sorush when he messed with Milandra," I said.

"Habriel apologized and laid the blame squarely on Milandra's shoulders. He said he was overexcited after a successful gig and had too much to drink. The usual excuses. He talked Sorush round. He said girls come and go, but best friends last forever."

"So, this best friendship they had was built on Habriel's betrayal and guilt and Sorush trying to shove down his conflicting emotions," I said. "That gives him a solid motive for murder."

"I don't disagree," Bertoli said. "But they'd figured out a way to make things work. Besides, what could have happened that night to make Sorush act so harshly?"

"Habriel liked to mess with people, by the sound of things," I said. "Maybe he made a jibe about

Milandra that no one else overheard, so Sorush struck back."

Bertoli took a bite of his cake and chewed. "I don't know. I can't see it happening now, not after so much time has passed. He was angry about it when it first happened, but it was a long time ago."

"What about Tabris?" Zandra asked. "Sorush called him a freak show."

"He's not! Tabris is a good guy, and he genuinely looks out for all of us. He's got a natural healing energy about him."

"But there's something in his personal life that makes him stand out?" I asked.

Bertoli took his time formulating a reply. So long that I'd finished my food. "This happened a while ago, and we thought it was over, but recently, we learned Tabris has been hiding things from us. Something he shouldn't have gone back to because he knows the risk."

"What things are we talking about?" I asked.

"Tabris is open-minded, and he sees the person rather than the gender. He's also curious about the world and how other people live in it. He often goes off exploring, spending a few weeks in other communities to see how things are run."

"Much like your old tutor, Dina," I said.

Bertoli's eyebrows shot up. "Yes! How do you know about her?"

"That's a story for another time," I said. "Go on. What situation did Tabris find himself in that wasn't approved of?"

"Angels can be narrow-minded," Bertoli said. "I'm not! Or at least I try not to be. Not anymore.

211

But Tabris decided to spend a month living in a non-magical community. These weren't magic users who'd renounced their abilities, but actual regular people with no knowledge and no ability to cast even the most basic spell."

"Tabris met someone there he liked?" Zandra asked.

Bertoli nodded. "We all know the risks of interacting too closely with those who have no understanding or awareness of what we can do. But Tabris fell for a regular girl. He got really into her."

"Which would have been difficult," I said. "He'd have needed to hide his true face and powers. Concealment spells hide wings, but he must have been uncomfortable not being able to use them."

"Tabris struggled, but he told the girl that he worked away so he could get a break from using magic to hide his true nature."

"Things got serious?" I asked. "Tabris was considering telling this girl he's an angel?"

"Yes, and that's when the problems arose," Bertoli said. "It's not encouraged, but it's not illegal for us to have relationships with those who don't have magic. But Tabris went to the higher angels and asked for their approval so he could marry her. It went badly. So badly, Tabris was almost arrested."

"The higher angels can be strange," I said. "But I understand their desire to keep us secret. Non-magicals can be cruel about things they don't understand. They destroy it rather than explore it."

"And the higher angels have much experience of that unkindness," Bertoli said. "They gave Tabris two options: give up the girl or give up his wings."

"Harsh. I take it he decided to give up the girl?"

"He had little choice. He realized how impossible it would be to pursue the relationship."

"Did Habriel know about this relationship?" I asked.

"We all did," Bertoli said. "Tabris confided in us when he was deciding what to do."

"It's possible Habriel taunted him about the relationship while you were all at the party," Zandra said. "Maybe he made some joke about it."

"It wouldn't be the first time he joked about something he shouldn't," Bertoli said.

"Tabris got angry. He loved that girl, and he had to give her up," I said. "It's another motive."

"The problem with any of us having motives is that we all have the same alibi," Bertoli said. "Hand on heart, we were all at the party together. Yes, I snuck out, but just to get your gifts ready. I was gone for barely ten minutes. Habriel was alive when I got back. And he was alive when we all left the party."

"We don't think it was you, but you should have been honest with us," I said.

"I genuinely forgot. I'm sorry."

"Give us more cake, and we'll forgive you," Zandra said.

Bertoli heaped our plates again.

"One of your friends must have snuck out of the hotel after the party ended," I said. "It's the only logical explanation."

"I know I'm not supposed to be involved in this investigation," Bertoli said, "but I've been asking around. Nobody could have snuck out of the hotel without being noticed. Lizzie said she was there all night. And we discounted the use of any windows."

"Which leads us exactly nowhere," Zandra said. "We have more motives, but there's still no opportunity."

Bertoli sighed as he cut another slice of cake for himself. "How could any of us have done it when we were all together?"

❦ ❦

After our delicious, if somewhat perplexing, talk with Bertoli, we were walking home to see if Tempest and Wiggles were at a loose end and wanted to hang out when there was a flurry of activity overhead. Cythera shot past. She landed outside the Sleepy Stardust Sanctuary and marched inside.

"What's she up to?" I hopped onto Zandra's shoulder, and we headed to the hotel.

When we got into the lobby, all our suspects were there, along with Lizzie. Cythera was inspecting something sitting on the desk.

Lizzie looked up. "I was about to get in touch with you. We found something. Or rather, Sorush did."

Cythera looked over and scowled. "I'm not interfering, but I was called to see this. I needed to check its authenticity."

I leaned closer to see Cythera inspecting an aged leather-bound book, the pages full of arcane script.

"It's the second missing book from our party," Sorush said.

"Lizzie said you found it?" I asked him.

"Yes, I was going through Nisroc's things, and there it was!"

"Where exactly was it?" Zandra asked.

"Buried at the bottom of his carryall," Sorush said. "I figured I'd tidy his room and collect his things. I was so shocked when I found the book."

All the other angels nodded along.

"This is a significant find," Tabris said. "Nisroc must have taken both books, but Habriel caught him. They argued, Habriel snatched a book away, so Nisroc froze him."

"When did that happen?" I asked. "I thought Nisroc came back here with the rest of you after the party ended."

"He did! But he's the smallest of the group, so maybe he found a way out. We were thinking through a window," Sorush said.

I glanced at Virgil and Arioch. Although they were nodding along, they seemed less enthusiastic about this theory.

"Nisroc finally stood up to Habriel," Tabris said. "Habriel was so rough on him at the Academy."

"It took him long enough to grow a backbone," Sorush said. "Although I never expected this would be the outcome."

"Nisroc is a thief and a killer," Tabris said. "There you go. You have your solution."

The angels looked at me and Zandra as if they expected us to agree, snap our toe beans together, and close the case. Something felt off to me. Habriel was killed, and at first, none of the angels had any idea what happened. But as we'd poked around,

Nisroc's name was thrown into the mix as the killer. Then he was killed, and they turned toward Bertoli, suggesting he was involved. When they realized we weren't convinced by that idea, the second missing book conveniently shows up in Nisroc's belongings, leading us back to him.

I wasn't a fan of coincidences, and this one seemed particularly stinky and unappealing. In fact, it stank like a week-old turkey carcass.

"It's the other missing book." Cythera stepped back. "I've seen it before, so I know it's authentic."

"Thanks for checking," I said. "But we'll take it from here."

Cythera stiffened. "Will you finally close the case? This is, unfortunately, proof of Nisroc's involvement."

"Would you be so good as to take Tabris and Sorush to your office and get formal statements from them?" I asked.

"I'm not your assistant!"

"No, but we need all the paperwork in order to record this new evidence," I said. "And nobody does paperwork quite like you."

She scowled at me then gathered the two angels, and they left, leaving us with Arioch and Virgil.

"Shouldn't we go with them?" Arioch asked. "Don't you need information from us, too?"

"Not yet. Your silence is fascinating to me," I said. "Were you there when Sorush discovered the book among Nisroc's things?"

"No, he called us into the room as soon as he found it," Arioch said.

"Is this the first time any of you have gone through Nisroc's things?"

"We figured we shouldn't touch anything," Virgil said. "But then Sorush announced he wanted to get things sorted, and we saw no reason to stop him."

"Do you both believe Nisroc is capable of murder?" I asked.

"It makes sense," Virgil said after a second of hesitation. "Who else could it be?"

"What about Bertoli?"

"Oh! I mean, it's possible. What did Tabris tell you?" Virgil looked at Arioch.

"We're not interested in Tabris's words, just yours. Every time we question one of you, we learn more secrets. Arioch, your use of gray magic gave us cause for concern that you couldn't be trusted," I said.

"You know why I had to use it." A scowl appeared on Arioch's face.

"None of us like that you use it, though," Virgil said.

"Somebody had to help Dina. I didn't see you lifting a finger," Arioch snapped. "She'd be dead by now if it weren't for me taking a risk and messing up my life by using a power that corrupts."

"You only helped her because you crushed on her when you were a student," Virgil said.

"We all had a crush on her! Dina was smart, funny, and pretty. You were always trying to impress her with your freaky ice magic."

"There's nothing freaky about my abilities," Virgil said.

"It's not natural to always set the dorm that cold," Arioch said. "Despite having two duvets on my bed, I was always freezing because you liked it glacial. It sucked."

The cracks were showing between all these angels. It had taken barely any prodding, and Virgil and Arioch were at each other's throats. Hiding dark secrets would do that to a person.

"Virgil, you hated Habriel because he took away your chance of success in the music business." I looked at Arioch. "And I think it's more than likely Habriel exploited your secret. Did he ask you to do things for him that you didn't approve of, threatening to reveal your use of gray magic if you didn't obey him?"

They fell silent.

"We understand why neither of you liked Habriel, but what about Nisroc?" Zandra asked. "What has he ever done to you?"

Virgil shrugged. "He was fine. Kind of invisible. Forgettable."

"Nisroc is guilty." Arioch gathered himself as he pulled back his shoulders. "Can't you accept that so we can get on with our lives?"

"That won't be possible. Nisroc didn't stand a chance against his killer, whoever that may be."

"I may not have liked Habriel, and I was indifferent to Nisroc, but I had nothing to do with either of these murders," Virgil said.

"Neither did I," Arioch said swiftly. "We were at the hotel when Habriel died. And we were all together when Nisroc went missing. We're not involved. You're looking in the wrong place. Sure, we have motives, but that doesn't mean we did it. Why would we pick now to do it, anyway?"

I sighed. They had a point, but I didn't trust them. "Go to Angel Force, and Cythera will take your statement about finding the missing book."

They raced away as if I'd invited them to a hot chocolate drinking marathon with a side order of cranberry chocolate cookies.

Zandra puffed out a breath. "What do we do now?"

"Now, we go back to school."

# Chapter 19

## School days

"Do you know how many strings I had to pull to get us an invitation here on Christmas Eve?" Bertoli fretted with his wings as we waited in the chilly corridor of the Angel Force Training Academy. It was the most prestigious training institute an angel could attend, and there was fierce competition to secure a place.

"You've mentioned it so many times since we asked for your help that I assume the strings you pulled were made of serrated metal, and they sliced into your delicate fingers." I was perched on Zandra's lap to keep us warm. The building was beautiful, but the stone walls were icy.

Bertoli adjusted the collar of his white shirt. "I'm just saying it wasn't easy."

I patted his knee with a paw and looked around. The grand building was made of pale sandstone and was something out of a wizard's fantasy world. The building had parapets, flags rustling in the breeze, grand entranceways, and it was all covered in tasteful festive decorations of green and red.

"This is a bad time of year to bother the Academy tutors. They're busy making preparations for next year's term," Bertoli said.

"Haven't the students all gone home for the holidays?" I asked.

"Sure. But that's not the point."

"The tutors have no classes or students pestering them. This is the perfect time for our meeting," I said. "Or is there another reason you don't want to be here?"

Bertoli fluttered his wings some more. "It's nothing. I just don't want to bother my tutors without good reason."

"We have a good reason," Zandra said. "All the angels under suspicion of murder came here, including you. Your tutors must have seen some of the goings-on. An impartial eye is just what we need."

"Are you suggesting I'd lie to you?" Bertoli asked.

"None of you have been completely honest," I said. "And I suspect your nervousness has more to do with what we'll learn about your student days than about us bothering your tutors."

His cheeks flushed. "I was a model student. They couldn't have wanted for a better one. I did everything I was told."

I snuggled against Zandra. "We'll see." Bertoli was always highly strung, but ever since we'd convinced him to get us an appointment at the Academy, he hadn't stopped fretting. He'd messaged five times the previous evening and again twice this morning to make sure we wouldn't be late and had dressed suitably. He'd insisted Zandra not wear jeans. My outfit, of course, was immaculate.

A small, smartly dressed house-elf appeared and bowed in front of us. "The Colonel will see you now."

Bertoli tensed. "The Colonel? I arranged to meet my old mentor, Major Hendrix. Isn't she here?"

"The Major has been delayed and didn't want you to be left waiting," the house-elf said. "The Colonel is free."

"I'm happy to wait." Bertoli gripped the edge of his seat.

"The Colonel doesn't like to be kept waiting. Please follow me. He is expecting you in his study." The house-elf turned and trotted away.

"Did this colonel teach you?" I asked.

Bertoli grimaced. "Yes. He's a retired warrior angel. He helped with battle tactics. He's not who we should speak to, though."

"We don't have a choice," Zandra said. "Unless you want to look rude in front of your former tutor. It's no skin off my nose who gives us the information."

The house-elf knocked on a door a short distance along the corridor, and there was a bellow to "come in" from the other side. The elf flinched but then pushed open the door.

I hopped off Zandra's lap and hurried over. "Let's see what this colonel is made of, shall we?"

Zandra was right behind me, and a few seconds later, a reluctant Bertoli followed, his wings drooping.

I entered a vast study dominated by a large desk and a roaring fire. Most unusually, there wasn't a single book in this study. But there were plenty of bottles of alcohol set on a trolley, from which the Colonel was helping himself.

He turned and waved a glass in our direction. "Too early for a snifter?"

"Greetings," I said. "I'll pass."

"Same here," Zandra said.

The Colonel was a huge angel. I'd never met a small one, but he was a giant of a supernatural. His face was craggy, his blond hair cut military short, and he was missing one wing.

He saw me looking and shrugged. "An old war wound. It ended my fighting career, but then I was offered a position here. It's tedious work, but the pay is good, and there's lots of vacation time, so I got stuck in and made the best of things. Isn't that right, Bartholomew? Where is that boy? I thought he wanted to talk to a tutor."

Bertoli shuffled into the room. "It's good to see you again, Colonel Morden."

"Yes, yes. That's enough flowery talk. Take a seat. I hear there's been bad business involving some of our angels, and you need me to solve the problem."

"I sent you the brief last night." Bertoli perched on the edge of a chair, while the Colonel made himself comfortable on the other side of the desk. We took seats next to Bertoli.

"Two murders," I said. "Both angels from this Academy."

"And they have the two of you investigating, is that right?" The Colonel waved his glass at us again.

"We're often utilized by Angel Force," I said. "I have extensive experience and knowledge, and Zandra has a keen eye for detail and never gives up a fight."

"Good skills to have. Well done, you. What can I help you with?" The Colonel's bleary eyes made it easy to assume this wasn't his first drink of the day. Perhaps the alcohol would loosen his tongue, and we'd get the information we needed.

I opened my mouth to speak, but the Colonel turned to Bertoli.

"How's the career progressing?" he asked.

"I recently made sergeant," Bertoli said.

"Only a sergeant? After all your Academy training? That's disappointing. You should be running your own branch of Angel Force by now. And I know they're recruiting on the battlefields over in Avignon, or are you still reluctant to wield a blade?"

"I'm happy with my career path," Bertoli said. "And I hope to have my own branch one day."

"One day! One day. That's no path, lad, just a wish. You don't get anywhere on wishes and dreams. You must act, man. Stand up for what you want and don't give up until you have it."

"Of course, Colonel. Thank you for the advice," Bertoli said.

"May I say Bertoli is an excellent member of law enforcement," I said. "He's always efficient and thorough."

"Who's Bertoli?" the Colonel asked.

I gestured to the squirming angel beside me.

The Colonel grunted. "So he should. He got his training from me. I can't be doing with that theory nonsense. I teach the practical stuff. That's the important part of the Academy's training. You can sit in an armchair and theorize all you like, but where does that get you? A few papers published, a gig on the speaking circuit. Boring and pointless. Hot air and windbags."

"Would you share some of that hot air with us while we talk about your former students?" I asked.

"Yes, yes. I know why you're here. Let's get on with it." The Colonel sucked in a breath. "Elf! Get in here. I need some files pulled. I teach so many young angels that they all merge into one. Of course, I remembered Bartholomew when he made an appointment."

I glanced at Bertoli, but he discreetly shook his head. "What memories do you have of Bertoli?"

The Colonel's brow furrowed. "This chap?"

"Yes."

He harrumphed. "I've always known him as Bartholomew. Changed your name, have you? These youngsters do all sorts of odd things."

"Bertoli is the name my parents gave me."

"I must be mixing you up with somebody else. Anyway, what can I remember about you?" He leaned back in his seat and solemnly regarded Bertoli. "A clingy rule follower. I doubt you ever broke a rule the whole time you were here."

Bertoli looked startled. "I didn't realize the rules were meant to be broken."

"Bend them, twist them, see how far they'll stretch. That's what makes you a superior angel," the Colonel said. "The pupils coming through the

Academy these days are made of different stuff. It wasn't like that when I was a student."

The house-elf appeared in the doorway. "How may I be of service?"

"Stand by the filing cabinet. You're to magic out the older records we need."

"As Bertoli would have told you, we're looking into his graduating class," I said.

"Yes. I got the brief."

"Two members of that graduating class are dead."

"The rockstar and the nerd," the Colonel said. "Apparently, they came to blows. Quite a turn-up for the books."

"Why do you say that?" I asked.

"Because the nerd—"

"Nisroc?"

"Yes. That's what I said. The nerd. Keep up. He was the type to scurry around the corridors in someone's shadow. He gave me the fright of my life one day when he appeared at my desk. I didn't even hear him come in. I'm certain he didn't knock."

"What was your opinion of Habriel?" Zandra asked.

The Colonel clicked his fingers at the house-elf. "The files. You know the graduating class. Be quick about it."

The elf got to work and swiftly hurried over with a file.

The Colonel flicked through it. "Here he is. Can't stand his music. And his personality wasn't much better. He was too proud. And too handsome. Of course, he had the charm to get away with it. There was a touch of the devil about that one."

"Did Habriel ever find himself in trouble with you?" Zandra asked.

"He wasn't such an idiot. No, he could get away with just about anything. Although, when his grades slipped, I had a word. I expect the nerd helped with that situation and got him back on track. Wrote a few of his papers, most likely. Wouldn't have had anything else to do in his spare time."

"You're referring to Nisroc?" I asked.

"Of course. Elf, the nerd's file. Now!"

The file dutifully appeared. The Colonel briefly looked through it. "I see here there was a brief period of trouble between those two. Nothing serious. Just high spirits."

"Bullying?" I asked.

"No, we don't tolerate that here," the Colonel said. "Habriel was high-spirited, and Nisroc was one of those types who preferred books to people. It was a personality clash, plain and simple. The problems were dismissed, and it ended after they left. And you're all still in touch, aren't you, Bartholomew? All still good pals?"

Bertoli sighed. "Yes, Colonel. That's why they were in Crimson Cove, which is where I live. We were having an alumni reunion party."

The Colonel slapped a hand against one solid thigh. "What a wonderful tradition. The Academy started it centuries ago, so I'm glad it continues."

"What about your opinion of the others in that graduating group?" I asked. "We know what you think about Bertoli, Habriel, and Nisroc. But there's also Sorush, Arioch, Tabris, and Virgil."

The Colonel clicked his fingers, and all four files appeared. "Tabris! That hippie peacekeeper. I heard he got into the woo-woo stuff, getting people to talk about their feelings and all that nonsense."

"I believe he's very successful at the woo-woo," I said.

"He's a tedious pacifist. I can't imagine him getting into trouble. Now, Sorush. Remind me about him." The Colonel consulted Sorush's file.

"According to Sorush, he was best friends with Habriel," I said.

That earned us another harrumph. "I can't see that. The facts in his file reveal him to be average. Another mama's boy, and clingy, too. Not made of the right stuff."

"And Arioch?"

The Colonel checked his file then jabbed a finger at us. "That boy had potential. He wasn't afraid to cross the line to achieve a goal."

"There was some rivalry between Arioch and Habriel," I said.

"No doubt. Habriel was the star. Arioch would have been intrigued by that. But I was more fascinated with his openness to risk. He would test the limits of his magic."

"Would that include gray magic?" I asked.

"The gray stuff, you say? It wouldn't surprise me. Arioch was fascinated by things we shouldn't look into. I'd hoped to recruit him as a warrior, but there was darkness in him. It meant I couldn't trust him. When you're on the battlefield, you need someone watching your back, someone you can trust implicitly."

"So they don't chop off your wings, you mean?"

"Exactly. Take your eye off the ball, and everything goes to pot." The Colonel looked at the last file. "Virgil. Yes, loved his celestial magic. Could be too intense with it. But he had talent, and he was a natural. I sent him on an ice mission to retrieve a missing artifact. That angel loves the cold."

"Did he succeed in his mission?" I asked.

"He did. Not exemplary, but competent. And they all graduated, so they had a degree of sense among them."

"Out of all of them, do you have any insight into who would be most likely to murder Habriel and Nisroc?"

The Colonel paused. "We can only do so much for these angels. We pluck out the potential and build on it, but if there is a dark seed inside, we can't cut it out. As hard as we try, they rot. I barely remember Nisroc, but the lingering feeling I have about him is shadowy. Never trust a lurker. They're always trying to find out something or get something out of you in a secretive manner."

"Do you think Nisroc is capable of murder?" Zandra asked.

"I suspect it was him, and then someone got revenge. Habriel was popular, so it would have hit home hard when he was popped off like that."

"It's a theory we've considered," I said, "but the evidence suggests otherwise."

"Recheck your evidence. Or don't you ever make mistakes?" The Colonel stood and returned to the drinks trolley. "Does anyone want a top-up?"

I looked at Zandra. She shook her head and wrinkled her nose. This conversation was getting us nowhere. It was also making Bertoli feel bad, since his old tutor couldn't get his name right and had called him clingy and a rule follower.

The house-elf returned the files and stood by the door. "If I may be so bold, it's time for your Academy tour. If you would like one."

"Yes. Off you go. I've got nothing else to tell you," the Colonel said. "Mark my words. It was Nisroc the nerd. Get that sorted, will you? The Academy could do without a double murder lingering over the holidays. Puts a bad taste in the mouth."

We were swift to say our goodbyes to the Colonel and followed the house-elf into the corridor.

"Has Colonel Morden always been so helpful and pleasant?" I asked Bertoli.

"I didn't realize we were seeing him," Bertoli said. "I'm sorry I wasted your time."

"This isn't a waste," I said. "I like nosing around old buildings. And we have the time. Where shall we start?"

"Bertoli! I'm so glad I caught you!" A high, tinkling female voice came along the corridor, and we turned to see a tall angel dressed in long white robes with a beaming smile on her face, hurrying toward us.

"Matron Maggie!" Bertoli stepped forward, all the tension leaving him.

Her intelligent gaze flicked to the Colonel's door. "Oh, dear. Have you just been in with Colonel Morden? When I heard Major Hendrix had been called away, I hoped I'd be in time to save you."

Bertoli nodded as he kissed her cheek.

"He wasn't too much of a horror, was he? People say he's mellowed with age, but I think that's more the whiskey marinade calming him."

"He had interesting insights into the case we're investigating," I said.

Bertoli made the introductions, and Matron Maggie smiled warmly. "It's good to meet Bertoli's friends. I hope you weren't leaving. I'd love to catch up, if you have the time."

"We were about to have a tour," I said.

"Let me show you around. And after that, you must come for tea in my rooms. You need warming up and plenty of food before you head outside. It's snowing again."

"That sounds perfect," I said.

This looked more hopeful. A warm welcome and an open mind were what we needed to crack this case open, help us get to the truth about this graduating class, and find what secrets lurked in these chilly corridors that led to two dead angels.

# Chapter 20

## Kindness and clues

Matron Maggie's small, private apartment was adorably furnished. There were only four rooms, which she proudly showed us. There was a tiny bathroom, a single bedroom just for her, a little kitchen, and a snugly fitted-out living area where we were sitting while she brewed tea and insisted we enjoy some festive food she'd set out.

"Is everybody warm enough?" Matron Maggie rubbed her hands together. "This infernal place leaks heat. I'm always saying we need more dragons."

"You use dragons to keep the Academy warm?" Zandra looked around the room.

"We have two per floor, and they're always kept busy when the students are here. Let me request Juniper's presence. She's such a sweet dragon." Matron Maggie lifted her hands and exhaled loudly. A few seconds later, there was a small thump in the bedroom, and a petite purple dragon, about the size of a small cat, marched into the room, her head held high.

Matron Maggie bowed to Juniper. "We have guests, and they need warming. Would you do the honors?"

Juniper inclined her head at us before striding to the hearth and blasting a flame into the waiting kindling and coal. Within minutes, the room was toasty warm, and Juniper was snuggled on Matron Maggie's feet, sound asleep after doing her duty.

"It's been a long time since I've seen house dragons," I said.

"I've never seen a house dragon," Zandra said. "I've read about them but only the super-sized kind."

"The Academy has an arrangement with the dragons," Matron Maggie said. "It goes back centuries. Anyway, I want to hear your news. Bertoli, you've grown into such a handsome man."

He blushed under her praise. "Thank you. I stayed in Angel Force after I graduated."

"And you're working in Crimson Cove now, is that correct?" Matron Maggie poured us tea and encouraged us to eat some of the chocolate delicacies. "I like to keep an eye on my former students."

"Yes, I just made sergeant. I know it's nothing to brag about, but I like my job."

"You must brag. I insist upon it," Matron Maggie said. "You were wonderfully diligent in your studies. You worked hard, while the other students fooled around. I knew good things would come to you. It always does for people who work hard and pay attention. Is this your lady friend?" She gestured at Zandra.

"We sometimes work together," Zandra said. "That's it."

"Oh! I apologize. I always want to see my charges happily settled. Is there no special lady friend in your life, Bertoli?"

The blush deepened on Bertoli's cheeks. "Work keeps me busy."

"Bertoli will find the perfect companion, I'm sure of it," I said. "And we enjoy working with him."

Matron Maggie cocked her head and studied Bertoli. "I fear the Colonel has gotten into your ear, hasn't he? That man is a menace. He's long past retiring, but he refuses to let go. Still, I can't blame him. What would he do with himself if he wasn't terrifying students?"

"He's an interesting character," I said.

"There's no need to be polite. He's ill-mannered and unkind." Matron Maggie clasped one of Bertoli's hands. "Ignore every word he said. He's only mean because he misses the battlefield. That's what he was made for, and it must be frustrating not to be able to fulfill his one desire."

Bertoli nodded slowly. "I know he struggles. He could be a good teacher."

"He lets his own troubles get in the way," Matron Maggie said. "And with only one wing, many see him as an outcast himself most of all. If he were a little less brisk, he'd be popular. Instead, he likes to reign through fear."

"Since he's an outcast, he should know to take extra care of the students who don't fit in." While Matron Maggie talked, I wandered around the room. Every space was filled with photographs of former students. The walls were also covered in older pictures, mainly group shots.

"You're admiring my montage," Matron Maggie said to me. "I have fond memories of every graduating class. I've been here since the beginning. And I intend to be here until the very end."

"You see an end to the Academy?" I asked.

"Everything ends. The world will eventually change beyond our recognition. It's the way of things. But I'm certain we will be here for many centuries. And I'll take care of the students who need a little extra looking after."

"Did you do that with Bertoli?" I asked.

"As I said, all the students. That is my job. And I was happy to care for Bertoli."

"What's this Survivors' Club photograph?" I pointed to an enormous group picture of students dressed in formal wear.

"Every graduating class has a huge ball to see them off. It's a last hurrah, if you like, before they set out on their paths. We call them the 'survivors' because not every student makes it to graduation. Some of them realize Academy life isn't for them, and they go on to more practical tasks. It's all valuable work. Just because an angel doesn't make it through the Academy doesn't mean they're unsuitable. It's a way of filtering angels to ensure they find the right way forward."

"Do you have a survivors picture of Bertoli's graduating class?" The sea of faces was overwhelming as I studied the wall.

Matron Maggie bustled over. "Would you object if I picked you up?"

"That would be acceptable." Matron Maggie's hands were soft as she gently clasped under my belly and lifted me, settling me on her hip.

"Here they are. Bertoli looked so handsome at graduation. Well, they all do."

Zandra joined us, and we studied the picture as we attempted to pick out Bertoli and his friends.

"There's Habriel," I said. "Who's the girl he's with?"

"Oh! That was a terrible business," Matron Maggie said. "That young lady was dating another angel in the class, but Habriel had a silver tongue and could charm anyone. He even charmed me a few times before I saw through his veneer."

"You didn't like Habriel?" Zandra asked.

"I like all students, even the badly behaved ones," Matron Maggie said. "But Habriel knew the effect he had on people, and he misused it. If he wanted something, he took it, no matter the consequences. I told him he could do better, but he laughed it off and said it was nothing serious. The whole point of life was to have fun, and if you weren't having fun, you were failing."

"From what we know of Habriel, he trod on toes to get what he wanted," I said.

"He did," Matron Maggie said. "And that angel there, the handsome dark-haired one with a scowl on his face, glaring at the couple, that was who the young lady was supposed to go to the ball with before Habriel swooped in and took her."

"Just like he did with Sorush's true love," I said.

"I believe so. And there's Tabris. That angel has a talent for soothing the most troubled soul. I've even used his services when I've had problems sleeping. He's heaven sent. Well, aren't they all?" Matron Maggie returned to her seat and set me back on a chair, Zandra settling beside me. "I was always cautious around Habriel. I shouldn't say this, and I should treat all students fairly, but some people give you a sense, and—well, you'll know about this, Juno—they make your hackles rise. You can't put your finger on the problem, but your instincts tell you to be careful. That's how I felt around Habriel."

"How about you, Bertoli?" I asked. "Did your hackles rise around Habriel?"

"We had to get along," Bertoli said. "We took the same classes and shared a dorm room. It would have made things difficult if we'd argued."

"Which means you didn't like him," Zandra said.

Bertoli shrugged. "Not so much. But not enough to want him dead."

Matron Maggie topped up our tea. "Although I was sad to hear the news of his death, I wasn't surprised. Habriel didn't believe in consequences. Our actions create results, and sometimes those results upset and hurt others. That upset can lead to an unpleasant outcome."

"When did you learn about Habriel's death?" I asked.

"We received word through the Angel Force network," Matron Maggie said. "I was upset, but then I got to thinking about Habriel and his hijinks. Of course, young angels are boisterous, but he had a darker slant. I hoped he'd grow out of it, but it appears the opposite happened."

"We've been investigating Habriel and Nisroc's deaths," I said. "We hoped to learn useful information by visiting the Academy."

"Oh, yes. It's such a pity about Nisroc. He was another young angel I worried about." She patted Bertoli's knee. "He was fragile. Most people looked out for him, but there were others who were less kind."

"You're referring to Habriel?" Zandra asked.

"Yes, when Habriel realized how easily he could frustrate Nisroc, he targeted him."

"The Colonel said it was nothing serious," I said.

"He would. His idea of a solution is to have a duel and the last angel standing wins. We all know how that goes. After all, that's how he lost his wing."

"The Colonel told us it was during a battle," Zandra said.

"Yes, a battle he insisted on having. Sharp words were exchanged, and he threw down a challenge. The other angel picked it up, and the Colonel was three sheets to the wind and didn't stand a chance. He's lucky he's got one wing left." Matron Maggie tutted. "What have your investigations revealed about what happened to Habriel and Nisroc?"

"We're convinced it was an angel from the graduating group visiting Crimson Cove," I said. "Somebody close to Habriel. The dilemma we have is they were all at a party together and then returned to the same hotel."

"Apart from me," Bertoli said.

"You'd never do such a terrible thing," Matron Maggie said. "Such a sweet boy."

Bertoli glanced at me, a look in his eyes daring me to make some snarky comment. But I had no desire to do so. I was glad Bertoli had been looked after by such a kind-hearted matron, especially if Habriel had been cruel to him.

"I would be shocked if it was one of my boys," Matron Maggie said. "They've known each other for such a long time. Why pick this moment to strike?"

"We wonder if the gang getting back together stirred up old memories," Zandra said.

"Do you not still have your annual gatherings?" Matron Maggie asked Bertoli.

He nodded. "Every year. We hold them as close to Christmas as we can. It doesn't always fit everyone's schedule, though. Habriel's missed a few years because he was touring."

Matron Maggie's expression grew stern. "Bertoli, do you know who did this?"

"No! I'm as puzzled as Juno and Zandra."

"I'm sure Bertoli won't mind me saying this," I said, "but he is loyal to his friends, even if there was trouble between them."

"My friends can't be killers," Bertoli said. "I know we've talked about it, but I just can't see it happening."

"Even with the motives we've unearthed?" I asked. "Arioch's use of gray magic. Tabris's scandal with the non-magical girlfriend. Virgil's jealousy. Sorush using Habriel to get girls. Do I need to go on?"

"Oh dear. You boys have been getting yourselves in muddles, haven't you?" Matron Maggie said. "I should have paid closer attention. Some classes bond instantly, while others take time to grow close. Some never do. I feel partly responsible. You were in my charge, and I let you go and didn't visit as often as I should."

"It sounds like you take your job very seriously," I said.

"Of course. My family has cared for Academy students for generations. You could say it's in our DNA. I tried as hard as I could with Habriel, but he was a bad boy."

"Do you have more photographs of Bertoli's graduating class?" I asked.

"I have hundreds of photo albums. Let me find the right ones. Help yourselves to more chocolate cake." Matron Maggie shuffled her feet out from under the snoozing dragon and bustled off into her bedroom. The dragon rolled over, blasted more flames into the fire, then fell asleep again.

Bertoli looked around the room and sighed. "This was always my safe place. When things got too tough, I'd sneak in here, and Matron would make me hot milk and give me a cookie."

"Exactly how old were you when you came to this academy?" Zandra asked.

Bertoli scowled at her. "You're never too old for warm milk and cookies. You try being in my class and see how well you do."

"My wonderful witch would have obliterated you all," I said. "She doesn't have your patience, Bertoli."

"That's true," Zandra said. "And I can see why you'd come here. Matron Maggie is comforting."

"She was good to me," Bertoli said. "She looked out for Nisroc, too, but he was too shy to bother her."

Matron Maggie walked back into the room and laid out an armful of photo albums. "These are all Bertoli's class. Now, who would like some Battenberg cake?"

We spent half an hour looking through the photographs, but I was only interested in the pictures of Habriel. When I'd looked at the photograph of him from the Survivors' Ball, there'd been a haze around his image. I'd wondered if the picture had been taken out of focus, but a closer look revealed the other students appeared normal.

While Bertoli chatted with Matron Maggie, I sat with Zandra, having her turn the pages, making sure she stopped every time a picture of Habriel appeared.

"What are we looking for?" she muttered to me.

"Difference. Did you notice the haze around Habriel?"

"Dodgy camera?"

"No, and it's more obvious when he doesn't realize he's being photographed. See this one? He's looking at his friends and laughing. The haze is really obvious, and it covers him."

Zandra squinted at the photo. "Maybe his magic is messing with the equipment. Magic and technology don't go together."

"Magic! That could be it." I looked at a few more photographs, and they showed the same thing. Habriel's magic was showing up on film. He can't have been aware of it peeking through. Yet it wasn't showing on any of the other angels' photos. Why would that be?"

I looked over at Bertoli and Matron Maggie. "What was Habriel's background? His family?"

Matron Maggie settled her hands in her lap. "He was a foundling. He showed up on the doorstep of an orphanage. He never found a successful family to be raised in, so he stayed in the foster system. He had a wonderful mentor, who encouraged him to sign up for the Academy."

"That makes sense," Bertoli said. "He never spoke about his family and even got snappy when I asked about them, so I stopped. It's no surprise he didn't want to talk about it."

"You know nothing about his history?" I asked.

"There was no note left with him," Matron Maggie said. "I wondered if that was why he could be unkind. He'd been abandoned as a child. It can leave a mark."

"I don't think it's that." My heartbeat skittered.

Bertoli peered at the photo album. "I don't get it. What have you found from looking at these old pictures?"

"Habriel is different, but not in the way either of you is thinking." I rested a paw on the evidence. "And we must reveal his true nature. It's the reason he was killed."

# Chapter 21

## Revelations

I sat on an empty desk in Angel Force, while the suspects in Habriel and Nisroc's murders shuffled into place. Cythera and Bertoli were there, although this time, Bertoli stood with the suspects. I'd filled Cythera in on what we'd discovered at the Academy and how the clues clicked into place after speaking to the Colonel and Matron Maggie and seeing the photographs of Habriel.

Cythera had grudgingly admitted I could be right and had put out feelers to see what she could learn about Habriel's background.

Tempest and Wiggles strolled into the open-plan office. They walked over and joined us.

"We thought we'd see the end result," Tempest said. "Oh, and Bilious and Ted are coming in, too. We met them outside. They got distracted by icicles hanging off the side of the building."

A second later, the higher angels floated in, Tinkerbell perched on Bilious's shoulder. They greeted everyone, taking their time and acting as if this was a family reunion rather than the moment we revealed the killer.

"It's getting crowded in here," Zandra murmured to me. "Maybe hurry this up? Tempest gets twitchy around too many angels."

"I'll be swift," I said. "But we must secure a confession."

"The way these angels have been turning on each other, we'll get it," she replied. "And we now know why the cracks have been showing."

"And why they've been turning on the more vulnerable members of their group." I glanced at Bertoli, who stood with his hands clasped, his shoulders tight. This wouldn't be easy for him, but he was part of the group, so he had to hear the truth, no matter how hard it would be.

Ted stepped forward and raised his arms. "It would be wonderful if we were here for a happy occasion, but I'm hopeful for a resolution. After all, it's almost Christmas. Nobody likes an unsolved crime at this time of year. Juno, have you discovered who snuck into town and committed these unfortunate acts of violence? A stranger, no doubt. Someone unconnected to the angels. Definitely not an angel, of that we are certain."

"There was no sneaking," I said. "The perpetrator is in this room."

Bilious looked stunned. "Did you not pursue our theories? They were solid."

"You made some excellent suggestions," I said. "Allow me to talk you through each of the suspects, so everything makes sense."

Bilious clasped his hands together. "This is troubling but exciting. We must visit here more often, Ted."

I looked at Tinkerbell, hoping she'd read my expression and help me keep the higher angels under control. She shrugged and wrapped her tail around Bilious's neck.

"Go for it while they're drawing breath to tell us the crazed candy cane did it," Zandra muttered.

I hopped off the desk and walked along the line of anxious angels. "At first, we had no idea who killed Habriel, but the more we talked to you individually, the more Nisroc's name was dropped, and he swiftly became our prime suspect."

"Which is correct. He'd had enough of being messed with," Sorush said. "None of us blame him."

"It made perfect sense. Nisroc was an outsider, and he didn't fit in. He was belittled and taunted by Habriel. Why wouldn't he want revenge?" I said.

The angels shuffled around. Several of them nodded. None of them looked directly at me.

"But it wasn't Nisroc," I said. "When we revealed our doubts about Nisroc's involvement in Habriel's death, you turned on Bertoli. Again, he'd been roughly treated and was considered something of a book geek."

Bertoli ducked his head.

"And that's nothing to be ashamed of," I said. "Some of the best people are bookworms. Although I prefer the term book dragon."

"How do you know it wasn't both of them?" Sorush asked. "Maybe they were in on it together."

"You'll know soon enough," I said. "All of you had solid reasons for wanting Habriel dead. Virgil, you were teased about your obsession with celestial magic. Your friends complained about your fixation with keeping the dormitory icy. And when we spoke to Colonel Morden at the Academy, he sent you on a mission because you're so adept at using that power. The power used to freeze both victims."

"It wasn't me," Virgil mumbled.

"And Arioch. Your use of unsanctioned magic, even though it was for a good cause, left you vulnerable. Who's to say Habriel didn't hassle you about that? Or he went a step further. If your secret had been exposed, you'd have lost your job."

Arioch ruffled his wing feathers. "I have no regrets. I'm glad I did it."

I nodded. "So am I. You saved a life. Tabris, your particular romantic interests made you a target. We spoke to Matron Maggie at the Academy, and she revealed Habriel got pleasure out of taunting others. As hard as she tried to change him, he only got worse. He must have found it amusing that you enjoyed the company of those without magic."

Tabris lifted his chin. "We cannot help who we love. Most people are too narrow-minded."

"You're correct. Your heart found a connection, and you followed it. But again, what if Habriel learned you were pursuing that relationship? He could have hinted that he'd inform the authorities. You would have lost everything, too. The higher angels had already given you a warning."

Tabris looked deeply uncomfortable but kept quiet as Bilious and Ted muttered to each other.

"Finally, we have Sorush," I said. "Habriel's alleged best friend."

"We were best friends!" Sorush said. "I was always at his shows, and the parties afterward."

"You weren't best friends. You were a fan," I said. "You used Habriel's celebrity to blot out a tragic loss."

"Loss?" Sorush's forehead furrowed. "What loss?"

"You lost the love of your life to Habriel. He took your girlfriend to show you that he was better than you. That's why you've never had a serious relationship. How could you, when you'd found a soul connection, but it was taken so easily? Taken by someone who was supposed to be your best friend, but he was anything but."

"While this is fascinating," Ted said, "I'm at a loss to know who did it. Won't you reconsider our idea that it was a deranged stranger?"

"Yes! Have you searched for a deranged someone hiding in town? Perhaps a deranged reindeer. Dreadful beasts," Ted said.

Tinkerbell whispered something to Ted, and he sighed and gestured for me to continue.

"The angels standing before us all have excellent motives," I said. "But we ran into a problem every time we unearthed a new motive. They all have alibis. The same alibi."

"Which means they're innocent," Ted said. "Juno, I'm disappointed in you. I thought you were on top of this case. We should have brought in another Angel Force division. One without such close associations to this troop."

"But we'd still have the problem of them being biased," Bilious said. "I could never convict one of my own, no matter what they confessed to doing."

Ted nodded. "Tempest, what about you giving this a try? You were our first choice to run this investigation. You may have more luck than Zandra and Juno."

Tempest lifted her hands, a smirk on her face. "You should trust them. They know what they're doing."

Cythera stepped forward. "Let them continue. I'm interested to know what their conclusion is."

That was a rare show of support from Cythera, and I happily took it.

"There were clues as to why Habriel was murdered. It started with Tempest's nose. As you all know, she's a skilled demon hunter and can always sniff out trouble."

Tempest shrugged. "I have my moments."

Wiggles puffed out smoke. "She's awesome. Can't be beaten. No demon stands a chance against her. Or me. We're a fearsome duo."

"That smell was the first clue all was not well," I said. "The next clues were discovered when we looked around the house Habriel rented. We found feathers speckled with gray and a bottle of hair dye. We assumed they'd been left by a previous guest, although I was surprised by that. Lizzie runs an excellent hotel, so must thoroughly clean the room before the next guest arrives. But at the time, we thought little of it."

Zandra reached into her pocket, pulled out the feather she'd collected, and set it on the desk.

There was instant shuffling from the watching angels, and several glances were exchanged. They knew we'd uncovered Habriel's truth.

"Then we come to Habriel's behavior," I said. "No matter how hard he tried, he couldn't resist stirring trouble. He enjoyed messing with people's heads, manipulating them, and getting everything he could out of a situation. Matron Maggie said he cared nothing about the consequences. He was a live-in-the-moment guy. But that live-in-the-moment attitude caused harm, especially to those he targeted. Nisroc and Bertoli."

"Which leads us back to them as the killers!" Sorush said. "It's got to be them. Arrest Bertoli. He'll tell you the truth. He always does."

"It wasn't me!" Bertoli said. "I had nothing to do with this."

"Neither did I," Sorush said. "Habriel was always making fun of you and making you scuttle off to Matron's office to cry on her shoulder, while we were left to see who'd be his next victim."

"Which goes to show, Habriel wasn't kind to any of you," I said, "even though you were supposed to be best friends. Habriel cared nothing for that. He saw you all as commodities he could use and exploit whenever he desired. Sometimes, just because he could."

"What does a feather and hair dye have to do with what happened to Habriel?" Ted asked.

"They're vital clues," I said. "Another piece of the puzzle fell into place when we met Colonel Morden, and he made a comment about Habriel having the devil in him. And then Matron Maggie showed us photographs of Habriel, and there was something strange about each of the pictures, particularly when Habriel didn't realize he was having his photograph taken."

"What was strange about them?" Ted asked.

"There was a haze around him, which suggested he used a spell or a potion to conceal something. What do you think that could be?" I addressed the question to all the angels.

None of them said a word.

"You all know the answer," I said. "Although I'm intrigued to learn who figured it out."

There was more tense silence.

Ted bounced on his toes. "I must know the answer. What does this all mean? Who is the killer?"

"Habriel was abandoned as a child," I said. "He was left on the doorstep of a children's home."

"I didn't know that," Bilious said. "Why didn't we know that, Ted?"

"I never thought to look," Ted said. "Why is that important? We have an excellent care system. The best in the world. Habriel would have been well looked after and wanted for nothing."

"Yes, and if you're an angel in that system, you grow up happy and content," I said. "But since we've moved to Crimson Cove, we've met angel hybrids who found the care system they were shoved into less than ideal. They weren't supported and looked after. So, imagine Habriel's confusion as he grew up surrounded by angels and was expected to behave like one."

"Behave like an angel?" Ted smoothed his white robe. "He was an angel."

I shook my head. "Habriel was much more demon than angel."

Bilious and Ted inhaled sharply.

"Habriel hid his true form with magic," Zandra said. "But using concealment magic for such a long time comes with a price. And sometimes the magic failed him, so he resorted to more practical methods of hiding. Which is why we found the hair dye and the feathers Habriel plucked out so they didn't mar his angel white wings."

"Habriel's demon side was seeping through, so he had to squash it," I said. "In a way, I feel sorry for him. He was being told he was one thing, yet he felt he wasn't. He must have tried hard to suppress his true nature, but it kept peering out. His bad behavior, his bullying, his meanness."

"Is that what I smelled when I came to Crimson Cove?" Tempest asked. "I knew I got a whiff of demon, but I couldn't find it. And then it vanished."

"The smell vanished when Habriel was murdered," I said.

"How extraordinary!" Bilious's voice was tinged with shock. "All this time, and we never knew the Academy educated a demon."

"Habriel was smart, but he must have been confused," I said. "And hiding what he was for so long was too much pressure to bear. So, I'll ask again, which one of you found out the truth about Habriel? What did he do or say that revealed his demon nature?"

I was met with the same wall of tense silence.

I stared hard at Bertoli. He looked equal parts confused and horrified by what had been revealed.

I really hoped my opinion of that angel was right, because what I was about to say could change his life forever.

"Go on," Zandra said to me. "You've got this. You know you're right."

I fixed my gaze on Bertoli. "Since no one is talking, and you all alibi for each other on the night Habriel was murdered, and for the night Nisroc died, then I can only assume you're all guilty. All of you committed these murders."

# Chapter 22

## You did it!

"Juno! You're claiming all the angels killed Habriel and Nisroc?" Cythera stood protectively in front of Bertoli.

"It's the only logical conclusion," I said. "They're all involved, and they're covering for each other. At least, that was the plan. But things started going wrong, didn't they?"

Bertoli looked dumbfounded by this revelation, while his friends appeared increasingly shifty, and there were several glances toward the exit. I tilted my head at Zandra, and she moved to block any escape.

"I've accepted the evidence you presented that Habriel concealed his true nature," Cythera said to me, "and perhaps through no fault of his own, especially when he was younger." She raised a hand to show she wasn't done speaking. "My inquiries at the children's home revealed Habriel's childhood was difficult. It was more than just the unruly behavior of a child who found himself without parents. The home said there were numerous incidents when he had to be separated from the other children because their lives were in danger. His records noted unangel-like behavior."

"And now we know why," Tempest said. "Habriel must have been so confused as a kid, being told he was one thing but feeling the opposite."

"Habriel was confused but very clever," I said. "He must have been quick to realize that, if he was to survive in that system, he had to become what they wanted him to be. The perfect angel. Or as good as he could manage. But sometimes, his natural desires won over, and he was unable to stop himself from causing chaos."

"He can't have been a demon," Bertoli said. "Angels and demons aren't friends."

"It's rare, but it does happen," Tempest said. "You should visit Willow Tree Falls sometime. We welcome diversity."

"So long as the demons behave. Otherwise, they get tossed into the prison," Wiggles said.

"They know the rules. If they choose to break them, they face the consequences," Tempest said. "So if Habriel was hiding in order to survive, when he got older, why didn't he break free? Find the right community and figure out what made him tick."

"He must have thought there was something wrong with him," I said. "After all, if you're told you're something enough times, you believe it. It's like when you're in school and a teacher says you'll never amount to anything. Hear that enough, and it'll crush you. You won't even make an effort. Perhaps Habriel kept hearing he was an angel and must behave as such. He thought he was broken, so he did the best he could."

"I didn't know any of this," Bertoli said. "I promise on my career. On my life, I just thought Habriel was difficult. Some angels can be prideful, and I assumed he had an excess of pride."

"Nope. It was an excess of demon," Zandra said.

It was time to turn the thumbscrews. "We'll make a deal with whoever talks first."

"You can't promise that," Cythera hissed.

"I'm sure none of these angels want to lose their wings," I said. "And it'll be a punishment that fits a double murder."

"I can't lose my wings," Bertoli said. "I'll end up like Colonel Morden."

"The same goes for all of you," I said. "You will lose everything. If you want to keep your wings, you need to reveal the truth. Did you make the plan together, or did someone lead? Who was the first to suggest Habriel had to die?"

"Hi. I'm not too late, am I?" Lizzie stood in the doorway, her eyes wide as she took in the scene.

"Your timing is perfect." I gestured her in. "Lizzie was working at the hotel the night Habriel was murdered."

Virgil sucked in a breath but was silenced when Sorush kicked him in the shin.

"Virgil, you have something to tell us?" I asked.

"We didn't do this," Sorush said.

"Since you're the spokesperson for this group," I said, "don't you want to be the one who gets saved? You know how seriously Angel Force takes murder. Reveal everything now, and your sentence will be reduced. You'll even get to keep your wings." I glanced at Cythera, and although she was seething, she said nothing to contradict me making promises I had no idea I could keep.

"What do you want me to do?" Lizzie asked.

"Sorry for the interruption," I said. "Just listen for now. As I was saying, we checked with Lizzie, and she saw no one leave the hotel."

"Which means we're innocent," Sorush said.

"Or does it mean you worked together to ensure she saw and heard nothing odd?" I asked. "You came back from the party as a happy group, making sure Lizzie saw you all. Arioch even kissed her under the mistletoe. Was it an innocent kiss, Arioch, or was there a hint of grayness to that smooch?"

Arioch slid a look at Lizzie but kept quiet.

"And, whenever people talk about Tabris and his excellent counselling skills, they always mention how calming he is. Matron Maggie said you helped her get to sleep, and when I first heard your voice, it made me want to shut my eyes."

"I've worked hard to be this skilled," Tabris said.

"Yes, we checked. You're skilled in hypnosis. Sending people into a dream state. Lizzie said she was refreshed after her night shift. And it was all thanks to your soothing tones, wasn't it?"

Tabris's jaw dropped.

Lizzie glared at him. "You used magic on me and then put me under? What about the singing? Was that a part of the plan, too?"

"Singing?" I asked.

"Yes! I forgot to mention, but I heard the most beautiful song drifting down the stairs. I crept up to have a listen, and… well, nothing. I thought nothing had changed, but I'd been messed with."

"Virgil and his perfect notes," I said. "They needed to get you out from behind the desk, so you'd be an easy target. Why not sing to you and make you curious? What tune did you sing, Virgil?"

"It was Sorush's idea," Virgil said.

"Keep your mouth shut," Sorush snapped.

"Nisroc was in on this plan to kill Habriel, too," I said. "I doubt it would have taken much to convince him the world would be a better place without Habriel in it. But then he had an attack of conscience, didn't he? He decided to come clean and reveal what you'd all done, which meant he had to die, too. You needed to save yourselves. Sacrificing one life for several wouldn't have been a hard decision to make."

Virgil had edged closer to Arioch, as if needing his support. "It really was Sorush's idea."

"Stop talking!" Sorush yelled. "It wasn't me."

"You hated him!" Virgil said.

"So did you. You went green with envy every time one of his songs came on. You despised the fact our tutors doted on him and ignored you."

"That would have been the demon inside of him," Tempest said. "They can be charming. It's an almost addictive quality. Habriel probably wasn't the better singer, but his charm convinced them otherwise."

"I knew it!" Virgil said. "My range was so much better than his. I couldn't understand why the tutors kept favoring him. Now, it makes sense. I was right. It should have been me!"

"It really does make sense," I said. "Sorush, since the blame is now being laid on your shoulders, is there anything you want to say to prove you're innocent? Perhaps implicate another angel?"

Sorush's face was pale. "It... it was Virgil and Arioch. They're always whispering in corners and making plans. They came up with the idea. I didn't want to do it, but they forced me. They said they'd tell my employer I messed around with some drunk groupies at one of Habriel's after-parties."

"Did you?" I asked.

"Maybe. But you don't go to an after-party just to get your T-shirt autographed."

"I'm saddened to hear this blaming game," Tabris said. "I work hard to keep the group stable, but it's a challenge. Habriel enjoyed unsettling things. Everyone would be content, and then he'd drop in a snarky comment and I'd be back to square one. It's exhausting being a part of this group, but I don't want to abandon my old friends."

"Which gives you the perfect reason for also wanting Habriel dead," I said.

"I'm a trained professional. I easily handle conflict," Tabris said. "I had nothing to do with either of these murders."

"Lies!" Virgil yelled.

"He was there, too," Sorush sneered.

"I was not." Tabris's wings flared. "You're the guilty party. You shouldn't drag us down with you. We should all name Sorush now and get this over with."

There was silence as the angels glared at each other, and then they all talked at once. Names were yelled, fingers pointed, and it was impossible to get a word in. Virgil and Arioch had paired up, blaming first Sorush and then Tabris.

Tabris began by accusing Sorush, but when he realized Virgil and Arioch had turned on him, he included them as the guilty party, too.

Throughout all the yelling, Bertoli stood in mute shock.

"Silence!" Cythera demanded. "This chaos isn't helping."

The angels ignored her as accusations flew back and forth.

I nudged Wiggles, and between us, we conjured an enormous fireball and hovered it in front of the arguing angels.

"Unless you want to lose those wings now, you'll snap your jaws shut," I said.

The yelling swiftly died down, and the angels looked warily at the fireball.

"Cythera was asking for silence, and she'll get it," I said. "This yelling is only making things worse for all of you."

Cythera nodded her thanks. "Juno, please, continue."

I startled as she used my name. It showed Cythera meant business. "Sorush, you claimed you were closest to Habriel, so perhaps you were the one who saw the signs all wasn't right with your friend. Was it the gray feathers? Or could you see the haze of magic around him he used to conceal his true form?"

Sorush fluttered his wings into place but didn't reply.

We drew back the fireball a few inches to give them time to think without sweating too much. Still, no one stepped forward, making me realize that, just as I'd suspected, they were all guilty.

"Habriel was a bully, and he was losing control," I said. "He knew being with the angels wasn't working for him, which must have been why he got out of Angel Force so quickly. He followed a path that gave him a degree of freedom."

"If all of this is true," Bertoli said, "why didn't he just show everyone he was a demon? Why continue to make life so hard for himself?"

"Habriel got famous while everyone thought he was an angel. He must have been conflicted, wondering if it was possible to reveal his true self and still be accepted," I said.

"There are plenty of famous demons," Tempest said. "I have a list if anyone's interested. You may be surprised by one or two names on it."

"Habriel was making everyone's life a misery, and when you all got together at the alumni party, you must have seen a change in him. Until then, you didn't know how out of control he'd become."

"It had been a while since we'd all gotten together," Bertoli said. "Habriel missed our last three Christmas get-togethers because of touring commitments."

"But I still saw him," Sorush said. "He was fine on his tours."

"I don't believe he was. Perhaps you reported to your friends how difficult he was becoming," I said. "You figured out he couldn't be a pure angel, and you were all sick of being mistreated. It was the perfect time to strike, when you were together, because it meant you could cover for each other. And what a perfect cover. No one would doubt the word of a troop of top performing angels."

Zandra smirked. "Almost no one. But we sensed something was wrong."

I nodded. "You all went to the party together and played at being best friends. Then you hatched a plan to steal the angel books, giving one to Habriel and hiding the other in Nisroc's room in case things didn't go your way. And it all went wrong so quickly, thanks to Nisroc wanting to come clean. That was when you turned on Nisroc. He was your weak link, and when he broke and threatened to reveal all, you froze him, too."

"And then they turned on me when Juno and Zandra kept asking questions and refused to close the case," Bertoli said.

"They needed someone to take the fall," I said. "I'm sorry that thankless task landed on you, Bertoli."

He sighed. "Nisroc and I were never really in the group. They tolerated us, but that was it."

"Maybe you were never in their group, but you're in mine," I said. "You're a magical misfit. And that is much cooler."

Bertoli half-smiled, his chin lifting slightly.

"Someone come clean," I said firmly. "Whoever does will get leniency."

"I've had enough of this," Sorush snapped, releasing a ball of light.

I ducked, the scorching heat of celestial energy singeing my whiskers as it whizzed past. Sorush's surprise attack slammed into a filing cabinet behind me, melting metal and sending papers flying.

Zandra's voice rang out, sharp and clear. "Tempest, now!"

My eyes darted to the witches. Tempest's hands weaved patterns in the air, violet energy crackling between her fingers. The office lights flickered and died, plunging us into shadow. Only the faint glow of angelic auras and magical energy illuminated the chaos.

I leapt onto a nearby desk, scattering pens and knocking over a World's Best Angel mug. From my vantage point, I saw Arioch unfurl his wings and summon a bolt of lightning.

"Watch out!" I yowled, but my warning came too late.

The lightning arced toward Zandra. She threw up a hasty shield, but the force of the blast sent her careening into a shelf. Tomes of celestial lore rained down around her.

A growl erupted from beneath an overturned chair. Wiggles, all snarling teeth and burning red eyes, launched himself at Arioch's ankles. The hellhound was small, but his infernal bite packed a punch. Arioch howled, momentarily distracted.

I seized my chance, springing from the desk onto Sorush's back. My claws sank into his clothing, and magical energy surged through my paws, making Sorush's knees buckle.

He snarled, reaching to grab me. But I was quicker, leaping away as a blast of witch-fire from Tempest engulfed the angel.

The air swirled with ash, magic, and the acrid scent of singed feathers. Zandra was back on her feet, chanting words of power. Office supplies lifted into the air, swirling in a vortex of improvised projectiles.

"Juno, get clear!" she shouted. "This could get messy."

I darted under a desk, my tail barely escaping as a stapler whizzed by at lethal velocity. From my shelter, I watched as the maelstrom battered the angels. They raised their arms, light forming a protective bubble around them.

Wiggles skidded to a stop beside me, his tongue lolling out in a hellish grin. "This is some Christmas party."

A deafening crack split the air as the angels' shield shattered under Zandra and Tempest's combined assault.

"Stand down!" Cythera commanded. "This is not the way we teach you to behave."

For a moment, the only sound was the settling of debris and our collective breathing. Then Sorush's shoulders slumped in defeat.

"We were doing our duty. Ridding this world of danger. We did it for the right reason."

I slid out from under the desk, surveying the demolished office. Scorch marks marred the walls, books and papers littered the floor, and the scent of spent magic hung heavy in the air.

I licked my ruffled fur back into place. "That sounded like a confession to me."

Several of the angels nodded, knowing there was nowhere for them to go. Bertoli's eyes were wide with shock.

Cythera kept her wings unfurled as she stood in front of the group and forced them to kneel. "You'll have to stay in the cells until all the paperwork is processed. So much for having a quiet, peaceful celebration. I hate Christmas."

"Allow us to take these pesky beings off your hands," Bilious said. "We'll keep them restrained over the holidays, and then you can deal with them as you see fit. You deserve a proper rest."

"That... that would be appreciated." Cythera looked over at him with surprise in her eyes.

Bertoli sat with the group, holding a hand against his head where he'd been whacked with flying office supplies.

"Just one moment." I addressed the angels. "If there is any goodness left in you, tell the truth about Bertoli. Was he involved in the plan to murder Habriel and Nisroc?"

Tabris raised his head. "Bertoli was never a part of our group. He was such a goody two-shoes at the Academy that we knew he'd never go along with this plan. So we shut him out. We figured out what to do and decided that, if it went wrong, he'd be an easy target to pin this on."

Cythera let out a huge breath before helping Bertoli to his feet and leading him away. He looked over his shoulder and mouthed, *thank you* to me.

The higher angels got to work, and I assisted them to ensure the culprits behaved themselves.

Wiggles trotted over and sniffed around them. "You sure know how to make Christmas interesting."

I checked over the angels' restraints before stepping back. "You'd better believe it. This was one heck of a gift we just delivered to Crimson Cove."

Wiggles wagged his tail. "Now all we need is a giant roasted goose each, and everything will be perfect."

# Chapter 23

## Festive fun

I was perched on the back of the couch, Wiggles beside me. We watched in contented silence as the snow fluttered down, adding a hint of magical perfection to Christmas morning. Vorana had hung twinkling lights in the window, projecting a warm glow out onto the snow and frost.

"Can we wake them yet?" Wiggles asked. "Tempest always yells at me when I jump on her stomach before dawn, but it's Christmas! She'll make an exception, won't she?"

"Patience, Wiggles. Let our witches rest. They battled hard yesterday and need to recharge." I was excited too, but two grumpy, powerful witches wouldn't be fun to spend time with, and I wanted this Christmas Day to be perfect. The last few months in Crimson Cove had been stressful, but this day would be all about family, friends, food, and fun. No drama allowed.

"I hear someone!" Wiggles' ears pricked up.

"It's Sage, floating down the stairs," I murmured. "She does that to avoid her harness clanking on the wood and rousing Vorana. Let's meet her in the kitchen. Vorana always puts down excellent snacks, and according to Sage, she goes the extra mile during the holidays."

Wiggles bounced off the back of the couch before I'd even finished speaking and trotted toward the kitchen, his stubby tail wagging at the prospect of treats.

I took my time, having a big stretch and shaking out my fur. At last, Crimson Cove was at peace. All the bad angels had been caught, and there was nothing to worry about. I was about to leap off the couch and join the others when a figure appeared outside the house, their arms stacked with trays. It was only just growing light outside, but from the white outfit, it was an angel. It was Bertoli! He didn't move up the path, just stood there, staring at the house. What was he doing?

I hurried to the front door, using my teeth and paws to undo the locks. I inched the door open, letting in a freezing blast of air. I stepped outside just as Bertoli turned away.

"Greetings. Merry Christmas," I called out.

He froze then turned back, indecision wavering across his face. He looked tired, suggesting he hadn't slept last night. I didn't blame him, since his oldest friends were lingering in cells for double murder after having attempted to frame him for the crimes.

"Is there something I can help you with?" I asked.

"I... I didn't know what to do with all this food," he said. "I made it for the lunch today. Well, we were having breakfast, lunch, and dinner together.

And snacks in between. But there's no one to eat it." Bertoli looked at the six trays of food. "I thought about taking it to the cells, but I don't want to see any of them ever again. Not after what they did."

"Come inside. It's freezing out here," I said. "And that food won't thrive in such frosty conditions. Neither will you."

He hesitated again then hurried up the path and inside, kicking snow off his boots before entering. "I know you've got people staying, so I thought you could use this. I was going to leave it on the porch."

"You'll do no such thing," I said.

His expression dropped. "It's great food. You tasted some of it, so you know I can cook."

"The food is welcome. And so are you. You had your party with your friends planned, and that won't happen now. You can't be alone on Christmas."

"What's that awesome smell?" Wiggles called out from the kitchen.

"A friend and his excellent food. This way." I walked into the kitchen, not looking back at Bertoli. As much as I wanted to smother him with sympathy, his anxiety suggested he was on the verge of running, so I gave the nervous angel space to calm down and make a sensible decision.

I walked over to Sage's favorite spot by the back door and greeted her. She'd recently lost her favorite prickly mat thanks to the foster kittens, but Vorana had bought her a replacement as a Christmas gift.

She was still half asleep, looking grumpy. "Where's the food?"

I looked at the empty bowls. "Did you eat everything Vorana put down already?"

"I got hungry in the night. I always get snacky when it's cold." Her gaze shifted to the door. "What's Bertoli got for us?"

Bertoli loomed in the doorway. "I brought everything I'd made for our breakfast. There's savory and sweet—cranberry muffins, poached salmon, bagels, and eggs, which I haven't scrambled yet."

"Set down the trays and get to work at the stove," I said. "It'll be a wonderful treat for Vorana to wake up and not have to run around cooking for us."

"She's been so busy at the bookstore that she's barely had a chance to bake anything this season," Sage said. "Treats have been sorely lacking. My stomach isn't happy."

"I wondered why I hadn't been smelling anything delicious lately," I said. "Although it's good news for the bookstore, not so much for our bellies."

After directing Bertoli to where everything was that he needed to make breakfast, I nudged Sage into action. "We need to bring in our gifts."

"I tied a ribbon around mine," Sage said. "After I played with it for a bit."

"Vorana will be impressed. That rat you dragged in is only missing one paw and an eye. An almost complete specimen."

"You got special gifts for your witches?" Wiggles asked. "I only got Tempest chocolate, and I ate half of it."

I nodded. "A rat for Vorana, and I found part of a pigeon. I should add some tinsel to it. Zandra likes tinsel."

Wiggles groaned. "Now I've got to get Tempest something else."

"I'm sure she'll adore the chewed-on chocolate. Remember, it's the thought that counts."

Bertoli had stopped beating the eggs and looked at us, aghast. "You give dead bits of animals to your witches?"

"Of course! Although we've yet to find the right creature to make them smile," I said.

"How about you find them no dead creature?" Bertoli shook his head. "It's disgusting. They can't like those gifts, can they?"

"They should, although they're never grateful," I said.

"Maybe next time go with socks or a tin of cookies," Bertoli said.

"What's all this noise in my kitchen?" Vorana ambled in, wearing a red dressing gown and slippers, her hair messy. "Bertoli! Were we expecting you?"

"No. Sorry. I didn't mean to impose—"

"You're not imposing," I said. "You're my guest. And he's brought breakfast. All you need to do is brew coffee and sit at the table and enjoy it."

Vorana smiled warmly at Bertoli before walking over and kissing his cheek. "I'm happy to have an extra guest. Season's greetings. And this food looks delicious. You made all of this?"

Bertoli nodded as he got over his discomfort and was soon scrambling the eggs, toasting bagels, and arranging plates of smoked salmon.

Zandra and Tempest shambled out of the basement five minutes later when the coffee was brewed, both of them sniffing the air. Tempest was carrying the three kittens. There was another round of greetings and explanations, but no one seemed to mind that Bertoli had shown up.

He set the last plate of food on the table, stepped back, and gently thumped his chest. "Before we dig in, I wanted to say thank you for everything, not just letting me have breakfast with you. I'd never have figured out the angels I went to the Academy with could do this. And I was even more shocked they tried to frame Nisroc and then me for what happened. I thought I knew them, but I didn't really know them at all."

"You're welcome." I looked longingly at the salmon.

Bertoli inhaled as if to say more, but Tempest waved him to a seat. "Sit down and eat. I'm starving. And I get extra mean when I'm starving."

Bertoli still hesitated.

"We'll always help our friends." I gestured with a paw at the empty seat to encourage Bertoli to settle in. "And we consider you one. We've had our troubles, but you're a reliable and trustworthy angel. I'm sorry I made you believe I considered you guilty of the murders. I know your character well, but I had to stay impartial."

There was a knock at the front door, and Vorana went to answer it.

"I sent a message to Sorcha to join us," Zandra said. "She's seeing Denver later, but she'll be at a loose end during the day, so I didn't want her to be on her own."

Vorana walked back into the kitchen, accompanied not only by Sorcha but also a shifty-looking Cythera.

Bertoli leapt to his feet. "Is there an emergency at work? Do you need me?"

Cythera gestured for him to sit back down. "No, everything is under control at the office. I was out for a walk with Maverick when I saw you coming here. I wanted to see how you were doing." She glanced around the table and nodded a greeting.

"Pull up a chair and join us," Vorana said. "Bertoli's brought so much food, there'll be leftovers for days."

"I can supply lunch and dinner, too," Bertoli said. "I didn't have enough hands to bring it all over in one go. Not that I expect to stay all day. I don't want to be in the way."

Vorana's eyes widened. "That would be amazing. And you must stay. I'm embarrassed to say I've only done the basics. Business is booming, so I haven't had a moment to myself."

"Stop standing on ceremony, Cythera, and join us," I said. "We can celebrate a successful case closure together."

After making several excuses and coming up with nothing good, Cythera finally joined us, grumbling that she couldn't leave Maverick for too long.

"I know we shouldn't talk shop at Christmas, but are all the angels behaving themselves?" I asked her.

"Some of them are talking, but one in particular is being obnoxious and difficult."

"Sorush?" I asked.

She nodded. "I think spending all that time with Habriel did him no favors."

"But there will be charges brought against all of them for the murders?"

"Yes, none of them are going free. And there'll be a review of acceptance procedures at the Academy, so this never happens again," Cythera said. "We're open to accepting angel variations, but we have to draw a line. We'd have liked to run tests on Habriel, but given he's a block of ice in Sorcha's freezer, we'll never know exactly how much of a demon he was."

Tempest swallowed a mouthful of bagel. "I'd say he was much more demon than angel. And from the tricks he pulled, he probably landed on the chaos side of demonic ability."

"Mistakes were made with everyone involved," Cythera said. "We'll learn from this. In particular, we now realize our angels aren't infallible."

I almost fell off my seat in surprise at Cythera's ready admission. "With the right protections in place, your angels wouldn't have been so easily manipulated. They'd have seen Habriel was hiding under a powerful haze of magic."

"That magic wouldn't have held forever," Tempest said. "As his demon power got stronger, it would have kept breaking through until the demon was well and truly out of the bag."

"Which must have been how his friends figured it out," I said. "They saw the darkness under the white veneer and were appalled they'd been lied to all these years. And when they got together and discovered just how manipulative Habriel had been, they acted."

Bertoli shook his head. "They were my oldest friends."

"Were they really, though?" I asked. "You told us that you and Nisroc always felt on the outside. It's time to move on from your past and forge a happier present. And what could be happier than having us as your friends?"

Cythera snorted before helping herself to a muffin.

Bertoli smiled at me. "Thanks. I appreciate everything you've done. I won't forget it."

Tempest jumped up and stomped out a small fire one of the kittens had started. "They're getting better with their control. I think they're on their best behavior because it's Christmas."

"Have you decided to foster them yet?" I asked.

Wiggles stamped a paw. "It's not happening. It's never happening. They're staying here once we go."

"I could take them back," Sorcha said. "It's always quiet at work in the New Year, so I'll have more time to look after them."

"There you go. They have a new home," Wiggles said. "Now, we usually exchange at least one gift over breakfast. Who's in?"

We all agreed that was an excellent idea, and after we'd eaten our first plate of food, people dashed off to select a gift to give.

Sage nudged me with her head the second I got back to the table. "You've been so busy that I haven't had a chance to ask you about your magical stones."

"Shush! Not today. We're celebrating."

"If not today, then when?" Sage glanced at Zandra as she returned with her gift. "I know you've done something to your witch, so she doesn't ask you about them."

"Have I? I don't recall. We'll talk in the New Year and fix it then."

"That's cowardly."

"It's sensible." Today was about fun, not problems.

Five minutes later, everyone was ready to exchange gifts.

Tempest leaned over to Zandra and snapped the bracelet I'd given her off her wrist. "That's my gift to you. I couldn't figure out what magic was in that bracelet, other than that it's old, but it's a blocking spell, so I'm certain you didn't cast that on yourself."

Zandra looked down at her wrist and rubbed it, her expression shifting to confused.

"Let's exchange the rest of the gifts, shall we?" Anxiety pumped through me. How had Tempest known about my magic? And the spell wasn't doing harm., . It was making life smoother for everybody.

"I just did mine," Tempest said. "I don't suppose you know anything about that blocking spell, do you, Juno?"

"The gifts! Focus on the gifts." I looked around the kitchen, seeking out a suitable distraction, but everyone was looking at me.

"Now you're in trouble," Sage muttered. "And it's your own fault."

Zandra's forehead furrowed. "Juno! What did you do to me? You gave me that bracelet and said it was an early gift."

I gulped. Perhaps this Christmas wouldn't be so merry after all.

She glared at me then sighed before shifting over and scooping me into her lap. She kissed the top of my head. "Happy Christmas, you perfect misfit."

I uncharacteristically purred.

Zandra leaned in close. "But in the new year, you know what we need to do."

I snuck a chunk of scrambled egg she'd left on her plate and nodded. We would. I'd pull on my big cat pants and ensure our lives stayed magically purrfect forever.

But right now, it was time to wish everyone a very merry and magical Christmas. Until next year.

# Also by

**Witch Haven:** Welcome to Witch Haven, where nothing is what it seems. Meet four fabulous witches as they struggle with their destinies, deal with misfiring magic, murder, and the Magic Council.

**Crypt Witches:** Meet Tempest Crypt, a witch who swallows demons, and Wiggles, her mini talking hellhound, while you enjoy magical murder and intrigue.

**Lorna Shadow:** A cozy mystery series set in the fun world of a personal assistant who sees ghosts. Meet Lorna, her ditzy sidekick, Helen, and Flipper, the dog who senses ghosts, as they solve crimes and save the day.

**Holly Holmes:** An adorable cozy culinary mystery series set in the beautiful village of Audley St. Mary. Each book is full of treats, murder, and twists. Join Holly and Meatball, her clue-hunting dog, as they solve murders and eat cake.

# About the author

K.E. O'Connor (Karen) is a cozy mystery author living in the beautiful British countryside. She loves all things mystery, animals, and cake.

When she's not writing, she volunteers at a local animal sanctuary, reads a ton of books, binge watches mystery series, and dreams of living somewhere warmer.

To stay in touch with the mysteries, where the killer always gets caught, justice is served magic style, and the familiars talk, join her newsletter.

**Newsletter:**
www.subscribepage.com/cozymysteries
**Website:** www.keoconnor.com
**Facebook:** www.facebook.com/keoconnorauthor